MURDER AT THE FIESTA

A ROSA REED MYSTERY BOOK 9

LEE STRAUSS
NORM STRAUSS

Library and Archives Canada Cataloguing in Publication

Title: Murder at the Fiesta / Lee Strauss, Norm Strauss.

Names: Strauss, Lee (Novelist), author. | Strauss, Norm, author.

Description: Series statement: A Rosa Reed mystery ; 9 | "A 1950s cozy historical mystery".

Identifiers: Canadiana (print) 20210302453 | Canadiana (ebook) 20210302461 | ISBN 9781774091906 (hardcover) | ISBN 9781774091920 (softcover) | ISBN 9781774091913 (IngramSpark softcover) | ISBN 9781774091890 (Kindle) | ISBN 9781774091883 (EPUB)

Classification: LCC PS8637.T739 M8733 2022 | DDC C813/.6—dc23

ROSA REED MYSTERIES

IN ORDER

Murder at High Tide
Murder on the Boardwalk
Murder at the Bomb Shelter
Murder on Location
Murder and Rock 'n' Roll
Murder at the Races
Murder at the Dude Ranch
Murder in London
Murder at the Fiesta
Murder at the Weddings

"*D*o you, Rosa Mary Anna Reed, take Miguel Rico Belmonte to be your lawfully wedded husband?"

Rosa stared at Miguel with wide-eyed admiration. So handsome in his suit, his loose trousers with cuffs resting on leather loafers, a rose boutonniere pinned to the lapel of his jacket, the last button unfastened. The morning sun streamed through the colorful stained-glass windows of St. George's Church, filling the near-empty nave with ethereal light. The church, a stone structure, was older than any building found in Santa Bonita.

Rosa had to pinch herself to prove she wasn't dreaming.

She wasn't.

She was getting married!

It was Miguel's idea to marry in London and return to Santa Bonita as husband and wife. In his words, he'd waited over a decade for Rosa to be his bride already, and since they would be living in his home country, it was only fitting that they tied the knot in her home country.

Her parents, Ginger and Basil Reed, were exceedingly supportive, but that was something Rosa had grown to expect. After the shock of their engagement announcement and their plans to marry soon wore off, both Ginger and Basil were blissful in their approval.

Rosa worried that her American relatives would feel slighted, but they'd already gone to the trouble and expense of coming to London just over a year earlier. Rosa had been about to marry Lord Winston Eveleigh, who was left in the chapel, waiting for a bride who had fled.

They weren't likely to risk another potentially scandalous wedding, and besides, Rosa feared her Aunt Louisa and Grandma Sally wouldn't be in favor of her choice of groom, a man who, in their minds, came from "the other side of the tracks."

"What will your family think?" Rosa had asked of Miguel. "And your mother? I haven't even had the chance to meet them. They'll think you've eloped with a foreigner."

"Sure, they will be shocked at first—you're the first non-Catholic in the family—but they'll be fine," he'd said. "They'll love you." He squeezed her shoulders. "How could they not? I'll send a telegram letting them know the happy news."

Rosa wasn't as confident about their acceptance, but her fiancé knew his family, and since she did not, she'd have to trust him.

Ultimately, Rosa was convinced to proceed when Ginger had pulled her aside and confided that Basil had been having health issues, which was why he had finally retired from his position as a superintendent at Scotland Yard.

"Nothing to worry about," she'd said. "The doctor says he only needs to rest and take it easy, but I don't know how he'd do on an arduous journey to California. And he'd not miss your wedding, Rosa, for the world."

Her father was in his seventies, and though Basil Reed appeared as fit as a fiddle, Rosa had no intention of subjecting him to something that might change his health status.

Once Rosa had decided the wedding was on, she was thrilled and couldn't wait to make plans.

Flowers were ordered and a cake baked. She and Ginger found the perfect dress on the floor of Feathers & Flair, her mother's long-standing and successful Regent Street dress shop. The fitted bodice accentuated Rosa's trim form, with short sleeves capping delicate shoulders. The satin skirt flared from the waist, the hem landing just shy of her white shoes, her height lifted by two-inch heels. Her veil was traditional, tiering down her back and pinned to her short brunette locks with a faux crown.

And now, she and Miguel stood before the Reverend Oliver Hill, a tall man with stooped shoulders, graying red hair, and a perpetual smile. He'd been Rosa's vicar for her entire life, and it was fitting that he'd be the one to preside over her wedding.

It was so different from the last time she was about to walk down the aisle. Then the pews were filled with the fashionably dressed elite. Now, it was only Rosa, Miguel, Ginger and Basil, Reverend Hill and his wife, Matilda, along with Aunt Felicia and Uncle Charles, who had returned from their trip earlier than expected and who were acting as Rosa and Miguel's witnesses.

Rosa couldn't have been happier.

"I do," she said.

The ceremony was simple and precise, just what it took to make it legal and binding. Mrs. Hill took photographs using Rosa's camera.

"You are a beautiful couple," she said, beaming. "Your mum and dad look so pleased."

Rosa understood Mrs. Hill's unspoken meaning. *Compared with last time.*

But that was in the past.

She and Miguel were now husband and wife, bound by the authority of the Church of England and the law of the United Kingdom.

"I only wish that Scout could've made it," Ginger said wistfully. "He'll have to be satisfied with the photographs."

"He can come to California to visit," Rosa said. She loved her brother dearly, but she didn't know him that well. With twelve years between them, he'd spent most of her early childhood away at boarding school and was out on his own when she was in her teens. Rosa felt like an only child.

Uncle Charles and Aunt Felicia, an attractive couple who constantly made the news in the London papers' society section, offered their congratulations.

"Small and quaint," Aunt Felicia said, looking a little perplexed. "But it does the trick."

"It's just the way I like it, Aunt Felicia," Rosa said. "No fuss, no bother."

"Oh, but it's the fuss and bother that make it fun! But, to each their own." She gave Rosa a sincere hug. "I wish you both all the happiness I've had with Charles." She gripped Rosa by the shoulders. "There will be bumps in the road, believe me, but love and stamina will win the day. Fight for your love, my dear. It's worth it."

"Thank you, Aunty," Rosa said.

Uncle Charles shook Miguel's hand, and Rosa hoped he didn't offer too much advice. Rosa could hardly imagine what an English earl, such as Charles Davenport-Witt was, could have to say to an American police officer of Mexican descent.

AFTER A LOVELY WEEK'S honeymoon in France, a gift to them from Ginger and Basil, Rosa and Miguel returned to Santa Bonita. The newly minted Mrs. Belmonte was about to meet the elder Mrs. Belmonte, her new mother-in-law.

"I'm nervous," she confessed to Miguel as their plane began its descent into Los Angeles.

He gripped her hand. "I am too."

Rosa gave her new husband a sharp glance. She

knew flying was a white-knuckle event for him, but she worried that it was more than the fear of crash-landing that he was referring to.

"I mean, about meeting your family for the first time, as your wife. You're sure your mother will like me?"

Miguel settled his beautiful copper-brown eyes on her, but his dimples didn't appear. "I'm sure, Rosa. But she's an older lady set in her traditions . . ."

"Miguel!"

His dimples appeared, and Rosa relaxed. "This isn't a good topic to joke about."

"Maria Belmonte is a wonderful, loving woman. Opinionated, sure, but a caring person, and a terrific mother. You'll love her."

Rosa had no doubt about that. She wasn't so sure, however, that the feelings would be reciprocated.

*a*t Rosa's insistence, they took a taxi from the airport all the way to Miguel's house.

Miguel had protested, "That will cost a fortune!"

"My parents gave me American money for a wedding gift," Rosa said smoothly. "You don't expect us to take the bus, do you?"

Miguel blinked, and Rosa felt a thread of alarm. He *had* thought that. Money matters had never really come up when they were dating. Miguel had paid when they ate out, but often he insisted on cooking for them at his house, and now Rosa suspected he was counting his pennies.

Something she'd never had to do.

Ever.

Not that she was frivolous, she just didn't have to worry about whether she had the money to buy something when she wanted to.

They'd only been engaged for a week, and in London, Miguel couldn't understand the value of pounds, shillings, and pence, and paying for things had just automatically fallen to her.

A small bump. Nothing they couldn't work through.

Rosa had been to Miguel's house many times before, but walking in after three weeks—had it been only three weeks?—and as the new "mistress" of the house, she found she saw things in a different light.

The Spanish-style casita had terra-cotta tiled floors and ceilings, white walls, and cool blues in the fabric-upholstered furniture and framed wall adornments.

Miguel dropped their luggage by the door and pulled Rosa in for an embrace. "It's not what you're used to at the Forrester mansion, but I hope you'll feel free to make it your home." He kissed her deeply. "You're the lady of the house now."

"I just need to pick up a few things," Rosa said hoarsely, feeling weak in the knees.

Miguel released her, cupping his mouth to shield a yawn. "Oh, man. I don't know how those pilots and stewardesses do it!"

Rosa felt a yawn of her own coming on and turned away. "Not a job for me. I'd better get Diego while I still have a bit of energy."

"Sanchez is dropping Homer off sometime later, too. I hope they'll get along."

Detective Sanchez was Miguel's partner on the police force. He'd offered to look after Homer, an African gray parrot. Miguel had adopted Homer after he was orphaned in a murder case. The bird now spent some time at the precinct so he wouldn't be left alone too much. Homer and Diego, Rosa's brown tabby, had met occasionally, and neither quite trusted the other. In fact, Homer, with his ability to speak, seemed to enjoy teasing her pet.

All unpacking and planning for the future were put on hold as Rosa and Miguel gave in to intense fatigue brought on by a long day of travel. And poor Miguel had to go to work the next day. Chief Delvecchio had put his foot down on time away, even if most of it had been spent solving a cold murder case.

"Just a short nap," Miguel said, drawing Rosa into the bedroom.

"Just a short nap," Rosa agreed, though the twinkle in Miguel's eye hinted at a little something more.

SLEEP COULDN'T HOLD off the inevitable, and by late afternoon, Rosa was being transported in Miguel's 1954 Plymouth Plaza. The soft-blue, two-door coupe was certainly humbler than her new pearly white Corvette convertible, with its white-walled tires and shiny, soft red-leather seats. Rosa noted how Miguel resisted traveling in it with her. He had been firm about taking his car when he visited his family.

Miguel's widowed mother lived alone in the south end of Santa Bonita, in an area predominantly occupied by Americans of Mexican descent. She'd moved there from Los Angeles when Mr. Belmonte died. Miguel had explained that his mother had wanted to get away from the big city and closer to the two of her five children who lived in Santa Bonita, Miguel and his sister, Carlotta.

As Miguel parked on the street, Rosa looked to him for comfort but instead found her husband's jaw tense and his mouth tight.

"Miguel?"

His smile seemed forced as he took her hand. "My mother may pout. She does that when she doesn't get her way. Of course, she won't like that she wasn't at our wedding, but when she sees you and how happy I am, she'll quickly get over it. It's not like there haven't been enough Belmonte weddings. My three brothers are all married."

Rosa had the feeling Miguel had a history of doing things that might have displeased his mother, like many children do, but used his charm to turn her to his side. She hoped Miguel was right, that it would work again this time, but held her breath anyway as Miguel knocked on the front door. He let himself in, Rosa on his heels.

"*Mamá!*"

"In here."

Mrs. Belmonte's voice was terse and uninviting. Miguel shot Rosa a look before leading her into the living room. The bases of the couch and chairs were made of woven wood—Mexican style—topped with thin, brightly colored cushions, and there were woven rag rugs on the tiled floor. A small altar in the corner had a candle with a rosary draped around it. Next to the candle sat an image of Our Lady of Guadalupe. A crucifix hung on the wall above it.

Even though the two had just walked in, Miguel's mother didn't leave her spot in the chair by the window. There were no hugs or kisses—unusual for the expressive Latino culture—or sentiments of being welcomed back.

She said, "Have a seat."

Miguel took Rosa's hand, guiding her to the couch, where they sat close together. He smiled, but his copper eyes flashed with a look of confusion.

"Mamá?" Miguel started, "Is something—?"

Mrs. Belmonte held up a palm. "No, Miguel. I must speak first. I'm your mother, and since your father died . . ." She made the sign of the cross. "May he rest in peace. I'm the head of the family now. And when I'm gone, you will be. Not your married younger brothers, *you.*"

"Mamá, you are being very rude to my—"

Mrs. Belmonte's palm shot up again, her eyes blazing. "Do not call this woman your wife. You were not married in the Church."

Miguel stiffened. "Mamá!" To Rosa, he shook his head. "I'm sorry."

Rosa finally found her voice. "We were, Mrs. Belmonte, I assure you." Rosa's accent had strengthened during her time in London, and the difference between her speech and Mrs. Belmonte's Spanish accent was stark.

"Miss Reed, I mean the Catholic Church." Mrs. Belmonte set her dark eyes back on Miguel and softened her tone. "Miguel, I'm sure Miss Reed is a very nice girl, but you have your pick of nice Catholic girls. The Abello family has three perfectly nice girls—"

"Mamá!" Miguel said sternly. "I'm already married. To Rosa."

Mrs. Belmonte's thin shoulders pushed back, her chin raised, as she turned her neck to stare out of the window.

"Mrs. Belmonte," Rosa started, desperately searching for a way to appeal to this lady's heart. "I promise you, I love your son. I'll strive to be the best wife he could have."

Mrs. Belmonte turned, focusing her attention on Rosa for the first time. "You say you love my son, but you tarnish our family name by presuming to elope."

"I . . ."

"And under God, you plan to live together in sin."

"But . . ."

"I will accept you into our family on one condition."

Miguel protested again, "Mamá!"

"You must marry in the Catholic Church. Miss Rosa Reed, if you love my son, you will become Catholic. You will be a good wife and stay home to raise Catholic children. And under no circumstance will you live together before you do so."

As Ginger would say, *Oh mercy!*

Mrs. Belmonte continued as if she hadn't knocked the world off its axis. "We can announce your engagement at the fiesta tomorrow. It's little Margarita's birthday. You remember, Miguel? The whole family will be there."

Miguel's eyes implored Rosa for a response. It would be up to her to decide whether they appeased his mother or defied her.

She glanced at her mother-in-law, a lady who would be a formidable force in Rosa's future and a grandmother to any children she and Miguel might have. She was a woman Rosa wanted on her side.

There would be bumps, Aunt Felicia had said. This was a blasted boulder.

"Of course, Mrs. Belmonte," she said. "I love Miguel and would do anything for him. I'd be honored to marry him again."

Mrs. Belmonte transformed before Rosa's eyes. She smiled for the first time, her eyes brightening with joy. "Miguel! I'm so happy for you." She held out her hand, and Miguel helped her to her feet. "You will marry at St. Francis. I've already spoken to Father Navarro. You have a lot to discuss."

She turned to Rosa, and her arms opened wide. "Rosa, *mi tesoro!* Welcome to the family!"

3

The drive back to Miguel's house was chilly.

"Rosa—"

Rosa shot up her palm, in a way reminiscent of Mrs. Belmonte. "You said she would be all right with us getting married in London. You said nothing about her strong Catholic sentiments. How could you not know?"

"I admit, I knew she'd be displeased, but her level of displeasure surprised me." Miguel reached for Rosa's hand, and she let him take it. "I'm a grown man, Rosa. I'm not going to let my mother run my life."

"Really?" Rosa took her hand back. "I didn't see

you standing up to her. You realize we have to get married again? And that I can't live with you."

Miguel laughed as he pulled his car to a stop in front of his house, infuriating Rosa further.

"She can hardly stop us from doing that," he said.

"Yeah? Well, I can. I made a promise, and I'm keeping it."

Miguel scowled. "You can't be serious?"

Rosa opened the door and stepped out, speaking to Miguel over the car's roof. "I'm completely serious. I'm not leaving my aunt's home until we are married according to your mother's wishes. As far as anyone in Santa Bonita is concerned, I'm still Rosa Reed."

In seconds, Miguel was at her side. "Rosa!"

Rosa flashed her palm.

Miguel grabbed it midair. "You have to stop doing that. Under no circumstances are you to turn into my mother."

Rosa relented. She wasn't angry with Miguel, not really. She was angry at their circumstances, which, once again, threatened to become a wedge between them.

"I'm sorry, Miguel. You're right." She fell into his arms, her chin tilted up. "But I'm determined to honor your mother's wishes. She's going to be a huge part of our lives for a long time, and we want her on our side." She kissed his lips. "We've waited this long to live together. We can wait a bit longer."

Though Miguel and Rosa had made a case for a second wedding to happen as soon as possible, Mrs. Belmonte had negotiated for a date in four weeks. "A wedding takes preparation," she'd said. "People need enough notice to make time in their plans."

Miguel kissed the top of her head, and she melted into his embrace. "At least let me drive you to the Forresters."

As MIGUEL DROVE up the winding, palm-tree-lined drive to the Forrester property, Rosa's stomach was in knots. The two-story limestone structure with a red-tiled roof sprawled along a soft knoll, warm light shining through the many windows. The bright-green palms contrasted with the blue sky, and the surrounding flower gardens were expertly kept and in bloom. During the war, the mansion had been Rosa's home, her parents sending her there for her own safety, then again for the last year when she had come to lick her wounds after Winston.

It was during those first years that she'd met Miguel, fallen in love, broken his heart while her own shattered, and returned to London an emotional mess. When she had come back to Santa Bonita the previous summer, she hadn't expected that her beloved soldier would have returned too, and had made a name for himself as a police detective.

Her eyes burned with frustration. Just when she thought they'd finally have their happily ever after, it was ripped away from her again.

Miguel reached over to stroke her cheek. "It's going to be okay, *mi amor.*"

Rosa swallowed thickly but managed to say, "I know. I don't suppose you want to come in?"

Miguel made a face. "Your Aunt Louisa scares me."

"You're going to send me to the lions alone?"

"The lions in there love you. Not me. I think you'll be okay. Besides, I'm beat, and Delvecchio expects me at my desk at six tomorrow morning."

A wave of fatigue washed over Rosa. She'd just sleep the next month away, show up at St. Francis, then move in with Miguel. Yeah, that was *all* she had to do.

Despite his trepidations, Miguel carried Rosa's luggage to the door. She stood there waving as he drove around the three-tiered concrete fountain.

When he disappeared, she took a fortifying breath, knocked, then stepped inside.

"Hello? Anybody home?" Rosa's voice echoed through the empty tile-and-stucco foyer, which, Rosa noted, was larger than Miguel's living room.

Rosa's cousin Gloria came squealing down the hallway. Thin and energetic, Gloria had short dark hair like Rosa's that curled around dainty ears. "Rosa! Is it true? We got a telegram from Aunt Ginger saying you got married!"

Aunt Louisa, hearing the commotion, stepped out of her office. She wore a full skirt and a floral blouse with three-quarter-length sleeves. Her hair was pinned up in a roll, revealing earlobes decorated with clipped pearl-cluster earrings which matched the choker necklace on her neck. It didn't matter the time of day or where Aunt Louisa resided, she was always put together with confidence and a look of professionalism.

"Ah, the blushing bride," Aunt Louisa said. Glancing about as if searching for someone, she frowned. "Don't tell me you dashed away from this groom too."

Her aunt's lips tugged into a slight smile, and Rosa knew she was joking, but her heart couldn't bear the jest. She burst into tears.

"Rosa!"

Rosa felt Gloria's arms wrap around her.

"What happened?" Gloria hugged her gently. "Oh no, did the wedding not happen?"

"It did, and it didn't," Rosa said.

"It sounds like a story you need to tell over drinks," Aunt Louisa said, offering a tissue. "Let's go into the living room and sit for a while."

Aunt Louisa instructed a maid to take Rosa's suitcases upstairs. "And let Señora Gomez know Rosa will be joining us for supper."

Rosa leaned on Gloria then headed for the living room, a sophisticated space with low-back Scandinavian furniture covered with blue fabric and accented wood. A yellow rug under a glass coffee table contrasted perfectly. Grandma Sally and Rosa's cousin Clarence were there watching *Our Miss Brooks*.

"Hey, Rosa," Clarence casually said as he slouched in a low-back armchair. "Welcome back."

Grandma Sally Hartigan, a mentally spry lady in her eighties with white hair in an old-fashioned bun, was far more astute. "Turn it off, Clarence," she said.

"But it's getting to the good part."

"Turn it off," Grandma Sally repeated, then

patted the cushion beside her. "Rosa, come sit by me, and tell me what's wrong."

"She got married, and she didn't," Gloria said glibly. "I'll pour the drinks."

Clarence chuckled. "This I gotta hear."

Drinks were poured, and Rosa relaxed a little after her first sip. Making things even better, her brown tabby made a languid entrance, giving Rosa an annoyed look.

"Diego! I've missed you."

She swooped him up and rubbed her face in his furry neck. "Don't be cross," she said. "I came back as soon as I could."

"We all knew you were coming back," Aunt Louisa said. She crossed her legs, her full crinoline showing. "We just didn't think you were coming back *here*."

"Without your groom," Sally added.

"It's Miguel's mother," Rosa began. "She wants a Catholic wedding. So, good news! You're all invited!"

"Third time's a charm," Clarence said. Recently divorced, he shared a daughter with his former wife, and Rosa imagined he was enjoying not being the center of attention when it came to marriage matters.

"My marriage to Miguel is valid," Rosa explained.

"I am married, but his mother doesn't see it that way."

"You're getting married again to appease her?" Gloria asked.

"Yes."

"In a *Catholic* church?" Aunt Louisa recoiled at the thought. "Don't tell me you're going to become a Catholic? A good Church of England girl like you? These arrangements aren't easy."

"We worship the same God," Rosa said. "And I know it won't be easy. The important thing is that Miguel and I will be married in his mother's eyes. She's my mother-in-law now—"

Grandma Sally finished for her. "She could make things difficult."

"Yes," Rosa said. Diego, seemingly forgiving her, had curled up on her lap. "I'm meeting the rest of Miguel's family tomorrow. His mom is hosting a birthday party for Miguel's niece."

"You know," Aunt Louisa started carefully, "you don't have to go through with this."

"What do you mean?" Rosa said. "Of course I'm going through with it! We're already married."

"And yet, here you are." Aunt Louisa uncrossed her legs and leaned forward. "All I'm saying, Rosa, is, if you've had a change of heart, maybe you could get the marriage annulled. I'm not trying to be cruel, but just look at the trouble you're already going through. There's a reason why people marry within their own circles."

"Mother!" Gloria protested.

"It's true. They understand each other." Aunt Louisa sipped her drink, then added, "I'm only thinking of your happiness, Rosa. Marriage is for life. You have to think about your future."

"That's kind of rich, coming from you," Clarence said. "You're still dating a ranch hand."

"But I'm not marrying him!" Aunt Louisa snapped. "There's a difference."

Rosa wasn't surprised by her aunt's attack on her marriage—Aunt Louisa had never been in favor of her dating Miguel and had forbidden the relationship when she was a teen—but hearing her harsh words still hurt.

Holding Diego close to her chest, Rosa got to her feet. "I'm really very tired. You won't mind if I go to my room now."

"You'll miss supper," Aunt Louisa said. "Señora Gomez is making roast chicken."

"Tell her I'm sorry, and if there's extra, to save me some for later. Good night."

4

Feeling very much like a tourist in her own home, Rosa reclined on one of the padded lounge chairs beside the Forresters' large kidney-shaped pool overlooking the sparkling blue Pacific Ocean. Her face tilted toward the California sun, Rosa could hardly believe it was only the beginning of March—the Santa Bonita forecast was for highs of seventy-five degrees. Her adopted, semi-desert coastal town was far from her homeland of England, and not just in a geographical sense.

American and British Post-World-War-Two culture couldn't have been more different. In America, pursuing happiness meant a lovely house, a car, and an updated wardrobe. In London, it still meant removing rubble from bomb sites and finding a row house to rent. Like Rosa with her Forrester relatives, British families lived together. Still, it was out of necessity rather than desire, and it certainly helped to stay in a mansion overlooking the ocean with a pool shaded by palm trees.

Ironically, it was not at all what she wanted now, as a married lady. Instead of awaking with her new husband by her side, she had awoken alone in a large bed with a fluffy tabby purring in her ear. Closing her eyes behind her cat-eye sunglasses, she watched the muted, dancing stabs of light penetrate her eyelids, making her drowsy. Adapting to the time change was difficult, and Rosa knew from experience that it took days. She wondered how Miguel was coping, having to show up for work that morning. She imagined copious amounts of coffee would be consumed.

As the mid-morning sun warmed her, a wonderfully soft curtain of sleep descended. In moments, she was with Miguel, in his house, and they were breakfasting together, sitting close, laughing at each other's witticisms.

"Oof!" Rosa let out a loud groan, rudely jerked wide awake.

"Diego!"

Her large cat crouched on her chest, his tail

swishing back and forth in her face like an out-of-control feather duster. He weighed nearly fifteen pounds now, a far cry from the shivering little kitten he was when she'd found him abandoned the previous summer.

"I was having a good dream," Rosa said.

Swiping Diego's tail out of the way, she turned her fluff muffin around and put her hand on his soft head to scratch his ears.

"Rosa!"

Gloria's cheery voice greeted her as she approached with two glasses of orange juice in hand. There was nothing like freshly squeezed orange juice; a luxury enjoyed when one lived where orange groves were planted. She handed a glass to Rosa.

"You're up early."

"I'm still on London time."

"I remember that hardship well," Gloria said. "Took me days to recover. Almost put me off going abroad ever again." She grinned. "Almost."

"This too shall pass," Rosa said, sipping her juice.

"Señora Gomez is making breakfast," Gloria said. "Coffee should be ready soon."

"That would be terrific."

Gloria eyed Rosa with concern. "Are you sure

you're all right? I bet Mom can arrange a thug to teach Miguel a lesson."

Rosa shot Gloria a look of alarm.

Gloria chuckled. "I'm kidding. I just hate to see you so down. Did Miguel really say you couldn't live with him?"

Rosa couldn't help feeling a bit defensive. "No. He wants me to, certainly. But Santa Bonita is a small town, at least when it comes to local gossip. His mother would find out."

"So?" Gloria said incredulously. "Are you afraid of her?"

"She *is* scary," Rosa quipped. "But truthfully, I'm thinking of my future. Miguel and I need Mrs. Belmonte on our side. A small concession and a bit of patience will pay off in the long run."

"You have more patience than I," Gloria said.

One of the maids approached with two cups of coffee on a tray. "I've made them the way you like," she said.

"Thank you, Darla," Rosa said, then sipped eagerly. "Ah, heavenly."

"I can't believe you're getting married *again*," Gloria said, her mind still on the subject.

"I can't believe it either."

"At least I get to be your bridesmaid this time." Gloria gave Rosa a sharp look. "I do, don't I?"

Rosa hadn't thought about the finer details of what her Catholic ceremony would look like, but she knew the American tradition. "Of course," she said. "You shall be my maid of honor."

Gloria squealed. "I'll help you with everything. Maybe I'll become a wedding planner!"

Gloria's career goals seemed to change with the wind. Since Rosa's return to California nearly a year earlier, she'd aspired to be an actress, an interior designer, and, most recently, a journalist.

"What about your position at *The Morning Star*?" Rosa asked.

"I'm still doing that," Gloria said with a sigh. "But —" She faced Rosa, piercing her with her narrowed eyes. "I just want to get married, Rosa. I want a husband and children, and—" She glanced over her shoulder at the mansion. "—a home of my own. Is that so bad? And here you've been engaged twice, married, and about to have your second wedding! I'm only asking for one."

"I'm seven years older than you," Rosa said, hoping to comfort her cousin. "You have plenty of time. How are things going with Mr. Wilson?"

Jake Wilson was a senior journalist at *The Santa*

Bonita Morning Star and had given Gloria a hard time when she'd started as an intern there, a ruse apparently, as sparks flew between them almost immediately.

"Slowly. I really like him, but Mother is being a pill. She doesn't think he's good enough for me."

"I rather doubt Aunt Louisa will think anyone is good enough for you."

Gloria's relationship with her mother was starkly different from the one Rosa had with hers. Gloria and Aunt Louisa were continuously at odds, where Rosa could always count on Ginger's support. One would never have guessed that Ginger and Louisa were sisters.

"What are you doing today?" Gloria asked. "Do you want to go shopping?"

"Actually, I could use a new dress for today's fiesta," Rosa said. "Something festive that honors the Mexican culture. It's a birthday party for a little girl, but Miguel's whole family will be there."

FEELING as nervous as she had on their first date, Rosa waited for Miguel by the fountain in the front yard. She wore the dress she had bought while shopping with Gloria, a flouncy number of red, white, and green, the colors of the Mexican flag. She'd even plucked a rose from the garden and pinned it in her hair. Gloria had approved of the ensemble. "I hardly recognize you as English. With your dark hair and green eyes, you look thoroughly Latina!"

Rosa thought so, too, until she saw Miguel's jaw drop.

"Whoa," he said, stepping out of his car.

"Too much?"

He laughed and pulled her to himself. "Not for me."

Rosa examined Miguel's face, pleased to see his eyes didn't look too tired. "You're doing well?"

"I snuck home for a nap."

"Good idea."

Miguel held the door open for Rosa, and she slid in. After stopping at the first traffic light, he asked, "Are you nervous?"

"Yes," Rosa said as she looked in the side-view mirror and checked her lipstick.

"Don't be."

Rosa scoffed. "That's what you said about meeting your mother, and look how well that went. I don't even know how to behave with your siblings. We're in-laws now, but I have to act like we're not?"

Miguel took Rosa's gloved hand and squeezed. "I

know. I'm sorry." He pulled the car to the side and stopped. After a breath, he turned to Rosa. "Do you still want to do this?"

"Do what?"

"Be with me? Be part of my crazy family?"

Rosa's blood grew cool. "What are you saying? Do you want to get out?"

"No! No, no, no! Rosa! I love you with all my being. I have since the day I met you and will until the day I die. And because I love you, I'd never want you to feel shackled to me. I couldn't live with myself if you grew to resent me."

Rosa's heart melted. The back of her eyes burned, threatening tears. "I love you too! And I apologize. How could I feel sorry for myself when I have someone as wonderful as you?"

Miguel pulled her close and kissed her forehead. "It's only a month. We'll please my mother, the last thing we do to appease her, I promise, then we can get on with our lives in peace."

"It'll go by fast," Rosa said, swallowing hard. She kissed her husband, then smoothed out the green and red layers of her skirt, preparing to change the subject. "Now, this party? Your niece is turning eight?"

Miguel's eyes flashed with relief, and he put the

car back into gear. "Margarita is the daughter of my younger brother Hector and his wife, Patricia. She will love the doll I bought her." Miguel tapped on the small, brightly wrapped package on the seat beside him. "From both of us."

"Sounds like a big party for such a little girl."

"Oh, the Belmontes love a party. No opportunity is missed." Miguel's brown eyes glazed over, and Rosa could sense that he was being nostalgic. "My birthday parties were always big events that lasted for hours. It was the same for my siblings. All the relatives came, as well as most of the neighbors, who brought all their kids. It's not like the usual American birthday party. The parents don't just drop off their kids. They stay and drink beer while talking over loud music. They don't go home until late in the evening after the kids are exhausted and falling asleep. There's lots of food, lots of singing, and of course, the piñata."

"My birthdays were a little more . . . subdued," Rosa mused. "There were presents and a cake. I *was* allowed to take sweets to school to share with my friends. It's just that I didn't get the full effect of getting those sweets from smacking a swinging papier-mâché donkey with a stick."

"I don't know how you made it through your

childhood without it," Miguel said with a grin. "Very cathartic, you know. Those piñatas are the reason I'm such a calm person today."

"Oh, really?"

They pulled onto a street paved in cobblestone that marked the beginning of the Spanish neighborhood and was also one of the oldest sections of Santa Bonita. Sidewalk cafés dotted the streets, advertising their menus on hand-painted signs in both Spanish and English. It was almost like driving in another country. Even the streets all had Spanish names like *Ave de Febrero* and *Calle Rio Bravo*.

After a few blocks, Miguel turned onto a residential street, *Camino Coronado*, and parked behind a line of cars stretched down the street. It was the last parking spot as far as Rosa could tell, although she couldn't see the end of the street since it gently curved away. The neighborhood was humble, with small but brightly painted clay-shingled houses.

Rosa gasped at the number of cars. "All these people?"

"Looks like everyone is here," Miguel said.

"Not quite." Rosa pointed to a red 1953 Studebaker parked on the street. "There's your sister and Detective Sanchez." Carlotta Belmonte had been dating Miguel's partner for several months, a turn of affairs Miguel had only recently come to accept.

"I had to tell them about the compromise we made," Miguel said. "When she visited Sanchez at the precinct, Carlotta was irate, and I nearly had to wrestle her to the ground to keep her from calling Mamá."

"And now?" Rosa asked.

Miguel grunted. "They're going to play along."

Rosa let out a breath of relief. She knew she could count on Carlotta.

5

*R*osa and Miguel approached the Belmonte *casa* alongside Detective Sanchez and Carlotta, who carried a small package wrapped in brightly colored paper. Rosa's doubts about her own flamboyant outfit disappeared when she saw Carlotta in a bright, multi-layered dress.

"How ya doin'?" Carlotta asked with concern.

Rosa hadn't known Miguel's sister for long, but she'd liked her right away. Carlotta's vivaciousness and earthy personality, together with her bold fashion sense, were a fascinating and delightful reminder of the essence of Rosa's mother, Ginger. Along with smooth olive skin, Miguel and Carlotta shared the same attractive dimples and shining white teeth. Carlotta's eye makeup brought out her beautiful brown eyes, always sparkling with exuberance.

"I'm all right, though the circumstances are strange," Rosa admitted.

"Welcome to the Belmonte family!" Carlotta said sardonically. "But in all seriousness, I've got your back."

Sincerely moved, Rosa said, "Thank you."

Detective Sanchez shuffled his feet and blinked his eyes uncomfortably. "Not sure what Delvecchio's going to say when he hears you're getting married in a month, Mick. He thinks you stayed in England an extra week to do that."

Mick was Miguel's nickname, used when he performed as the lead in his band, Mick and the Beat Boys.

"We *did*," Miguel said. "But now we're going to play along with Mom's game."

Rosa took Miguel's arm and caught his eye. "It's fine, Miguel. Let's try to have fun, all right?"

Miguel's shoulders relaxed, and he kissed her forehead. "There are so many reasons why I love you."

As they stepped onto the front stoop, Rosa heard the upbeat and melodic sound of mariachi music.

She took a deep breath to try quelling the butterflies in her stomach.

Miguel knocked on the door, but after only a few seconds, grasped the doorknob.

"No one is going to hear us." He shot Carlotta a knowing glance.

The music volume intensified as soon as the door swung open to an almost empty living room. A lone little girl, her dark hair tied with a red ribbon, wore a pretty dress and sat on the Mexican-style couch, her hands over her eyes. Counting loudly and slowly, she yelled, "Ten!" Uncovering her eyes, she raised an empty coffee can with the word "HOME" marked on it and waved it in the air. "Ready or not, here I come!"

She jumped up from the sofa and looked wildly about her, but when she saw who was standing just inside the door, she stopped in her spot.

"Yaaaaay! *Tío* Miguel and *Tía* Carlotta are heeeere!" She ran over to Miguel, who scooped her up and gave her a big kiss on the cheek. "Hey, *chiquita*! Happy birthday."

Miguel set his niece down, and she ran to Carlotta for another big hug.

"*Mi corazon*," Carlotta said. "Happy birthday. We have some gifts for you." Margarita's eyes widened at the sight of the packages Miguel and Carlotta carried.

"As you see, we have brought friends, but first—" Miguel waved his hand at the empty room, "If you're playing *las escondidas*, you'd better start hunting."

"Oh, right!" The little girl regarded Rosa and Detective Sanchez with a glance, then turned and ran at full speed.

Miguel yelled after her, "Where is *Abuela* Belmonte?"

Margarita yelled in return, "Out back!"

"Hi, Abelardo," Carlotta whispered loudly, wiggling her fingers at a closet doorway as it cracked open slightly. Inside, Rosa could just make out the form of a small boy, about six years old, smiling shyly at her. He wore a white, collared shirt with the buttons done up wrongly, his hair was tousled, and his shoelaces were untied.

"That one looks like a troublemaker," Detective Sanchez said with a chuckle.

"That's my brother Ignacio's oldest," Miguel remarked. "His wife, Josefina, does her best with the boy. I've watched her tie his shoes, comb his hair, and straighten his shirt. Ten minutes later, he looks like he just won a wrestling match with a bear cub."

Miguel thumbed his hand at Detective Sanchez. "He reminds me of a certain police detective,"

Detective Sanchez nodded sagely. "The kid is *obviously* destined for greatness."

They reached the door to the large wooden-fenced yard. A turntable on the back porch proved to be the source of the loud party music. A large group of adults was scattered about—sitting in fold-able chairs in small circles or standing in groups—all talking animatedly. Some were shouting over the music, and Rosa could hear snippets of both English and Spanish conversation.

"There's Tomás and Paulina," Carlotta said to Detective Sanchez. "Let's go say hi." She turned away, pulling the burly detective by the hand.

Hundreds of streamers, triangle-shaped and multicolored, hung overhead. Green and red Christmas-style lights hung from the roofline, decorating the window frames. A papier-mâché donkey with pink, purple, and yellow glitter hung from one of the lower branches of a large oak tree, also trimmed with streamers and glittering ornaments.

Long tables were filled with Mexican food, some of which Rosa recognized: empanadas, chicken taquitos, and nachos with at least six kinds of salsa dips. A generously sized punch bowl and all kinds of beer and wine were available.

Rosa had never experienced so much vivid color, frenetic conversation, and loud music coming from one backyard. She blinked rapidly to take it all in at once as she hung on tightly to Miguel's hand.

In his mid-twenties, a portly young Latino man holding a beer bottle pointed at Rosa and Miguel. Grinning broadly, he displayed those familiar Belmonte dimples. The woman he'd been talking to turned around to see where the man was pointing.

"Aha!" Mrs. Belmonte said loudly. "*¡Finalmente!*"

"Mamá," Miguel returned.

"Miguel! Come to Mamá."

Rosa smiled with amusement as Miguel bent low to hug his little mamá. Afterward, she held on to his arms and stared up with fondness. "You look tired."

"I know, Mamá. A lot is going on."

"Always so busy," Mrs. Belmonte said. She smiled at Rosa as if the uncomfortable first meeting the day before hadn't even happened. "Hello, Miss Reed . . ."

"Mamá," Miguel protested. "You can call her Rosa."

Mrs. Belmonte never skipped a beat. "Rosa! Welcome!"

Rosa shouted over the music. "Thank you."

Mrs. Belmonte focused her large brown eyes on her son. "We have set a date, *si*? Father Navarro has confirmed it?" She smiled like a woman who had won a large bet. "An April wedding is so beautiful. Not too hot, but lovely flowers in bloom." Turning back to Miguel, she went on, "But time enough for your band to learn some proper Mexican music, I think, si?" She turned to Rosa. "Meek and the Beat Boys, huh?"

Miguel had played little with his band lately. "I'll have to let the boys know that they have to borrow some *guitarrones mexicanos* and accordions." He smiled as he looked at Rosa.

"Don't forget the trumpet," his mom said. "Miguel used to play the mariachi all the time on the trumpet."

A boisterous voice from behind Miguel said, "Not very well, though!" It was the young, stocky man that Mrs. Belmonte had been talking to earlier. He clapped his hand on Miguel's shoulder. "Talk about your crime scene. Every time my big brother picked up that thing, it was a bona fide felony."

A chuckle was shared between the man and the woman at his side.

"Hector!" Mrs. Belmonte playfully scolded her son. "You will frighten, Miss Reed."

Rosa shared a look with Miguel. His mother had made it clear she would be Miss Reed to his family until the Catholic ceremony was over.

"Rosa," Miguel started, "I want you to meet my brother Hector and his wife, Patricia."

"Pleased to meet you," Rosa said as they shook hands. "You must be the parents of the birthday girl."

"Yes. And we hear you're to be married soon?" Patricia said, a question in her eyes. It appeared Mrs. Belmonte had announced the news before Rosa and Miguel had arrived. Rosa answered simply, "We are."

Hector wasn't as subtle. "A rush to the altar, huh? Another Belmonte on the way?"

Rosa was mortified. Her cheeks burned as she muttered, "I assure you . . ."

"He's joking," Miguel said, his lips tight. "But not so funny."

They were joined by another lady with wine-induced-blushed cheeks. "Aha. At last, we meet her!" She was taller than Miguel's mother, with slimmer facial features and dark hair with streaks of white tied in a tight bun. She was accompanied by a man of about the same age, who wore a casual, white-silk polo shirt with a bolo tie. His black but rapidly graying hair made him look suave as he casually smoked a cigarette. In his hand was a can of Tecate beer.

Miguel began the introductions. "And this is my aunt Francisca, sister to my father, Luis. And her husband, Salvador Vasquez."

"New to the family," Mrs. Belmonte said without smiling. "We haven't had time to *check him out*, as you detectives like to say."

"You're newly married?" Rosa said to the Vasquezes, wishing she could share in their joy more honestly. "Congratulations."

"Thanks." Francisca Vasquez smiled. "It's been three months now."

Salvador Vasquez gestured toward the rest of the people in the yard. He spoke in a low baritone voice. "I'm slowly learning how to fit in with *el clan Belmonte*."

"Like I told you at the wedding," Mrs. Belmonte said, a stern eyebrow raised, "as long as you treat Francisca like a princess, you will fit right in."

"Si, Señora Belmonte. I'm doing my best." Salvador Vasquez kissed his wife on the cheek, gave Mrs. Belmonte a challenging stare, then took a sip of beer.

"Oh," Mrs. Belmonte said, staring across the yard. "Mrs. Gonzales is here. She's my new neighbor."

Rosa followed Mrs. Belmonte's gaze, as it landed on an elderly Latina lady who had just arrived. "Excuse me, please," Mrs. Belmonte said. She seemed eager to leave their grouping and hurried away.

Rosa let out a breath. She wished she could hurry away too.

6

*T*he late afternoon passed by in a swirl of music, polite conversation, and a blur of new faces and names. Evening darkness was just descending on the happy gathering when a cheer suddenly went up. Mrs. Belmonte announced that it was time for the piñata, and after that, the cutting of the cake.

This was by far the longest birthday party Rosa had ever experienced.

The children were lined up, and the first child, a boy about eight, was blindfolded, spun around a few times, and given a stick. The crowd sang a Mexican folk melody at Miguel's direction while the child blindly tried to bash the piñata.

Finally, the fifth child in line, a girl with pigtails

and black-framed glasses, managed the direct hit that split open the piñata. Pandemonium ensued as another large cheer went up. Hundreds of pieces of candy wrapped in sparkly paper fell to the soft ground and scattered all around the base of the tree.

The volume of the shrieks from the kids and the shouts from the adults startled Rosa. Two dozen children frantically descended upon the base of the tree, tore off wrappers, and stuffed all manner of soft and hard candy into their eager mouths. To Rosa, the whole thing seemed happily out of control.

This was a long way from South Kensington!

The cake-cutting ceremony was even stranger to Rosa. The birthday girl had her hands tied behind her back, and then her head was gently but firmly shoved into the large, brightly decorated, and creamy-looking cake while the crowd shouted, "¡Mordida! ¡Mordida! ¡Mordida! Take a bite!"

This was met with howls of laughter. The eight-year-old girl gave everyone a huge grin, and then gobbled up the gooey mess.

Rosa had to laugh out loud along with everyone else.

"I think I will pass on the piece of cake," she said to Miguel.

"Mom has another one in the kitchen for us

grown-ups." Miguel took her hand. "C'mon, I'll take you."

As they stepped onto the back porch, the elderly lady that Maria Belmonte had greeted earlier was there, rocking slowly in a wooden rocking chair, barely visible in the fading light. She had a blanket draped over her spindly knees and a shawl over her thin shoulders.

"Oh, hello, Mrs. Gonzales," Miguel said, with a note of surprise

"*La fiesta acaba de empezar,*" came the sound of the woman's frail voice.

"Actually, the party has been going for a while already. Are you okay? I can get my mom to escort you home if you have had enough."

"I'm fine, Pedro," the woman said in a heavy Spanish accent as she smiled weakly. "You and your wife can run along; I can watch the kids for you."

After a wary glance directed at Rosa, he said softly, "Okay. See you."

The sweet-looking old lady smiled and waved.

Miguel spoke into Rosa's ear. "She's confusing me with her late husband. She likes to drop in for a visit, but according to my mom, she shows up at the door not remembering why she came over or where she is."

A piercing shriek caused Rosa to jump. She and Miguel turned to the source.

"What is it, Mrs. Gonzales?" Miguel asked.

Now standing, Mrs. Gonzales pointed a crooked finger. "A black moth! Just flew into the house." She stared at Rosa. "Bad luck. Bad, bad luck for all who are here."

Miguel patted the shaken lady on the shoulder. "It's all right, Mrs. Gonzales. Why don't you sit down?" He helped her back into the rocking chair. "It's very comfortable."

"How sad," Rosa said as she and Miguel went inside. "The mind is such an amazing yet fragile thing."

As Miguel had promised, an identical cake to the one outside sat under a glass cover on the counter. Miguel removed the cover and cut a slice for them both.

"Delicious!" Rosa said after a bite.

"*Pastel de tres leches,*" Miguel said. "Always was my favorite." He wiped a stray crumb from Rosa's chin, then kissed the icing off her lips. "Especially now."

Rosa cast a look about the kitchen. "Miguel!"

After finishing their cake, they stepped back into the backyard to rejoin the party. Just as it started to get dark, Rosa noticed a short, stocky Caucasian man with receding gray hair standing on the porch. Rather pallid-looking, the man had bushy eyebrows on a prominent ridge above squinty eyes. He scanned the crowd. Finally, his eyes landed on Salvador Vasquez, and with a nod of his chin, motioned for Salvador to join him.

A short conversation occurred between them before the newcomer disappeared. Salvador Vasquez returned to his wife, Francisca, and spoke into her ear. She looked at him with a look of disappointment as he turned to walk away.

"I think I have subjected you to enough," Miguel said as he put his arm around Rosa's shoulder. "Unless you want to stay for the fireworks. They start at nine o'clock."

"I *am* getting a bit tired," Rosa said. "I imagine you are too. Just wait until tomorrow. It gets worse before it gets better."

Miguel groaned. "Delvecchio isn't giving me any slack."

Rosa liked the gruff Chief Delvecchio. Despite her being female and from England, he had made room for her to consult with the Santa Bonita Police, proving to be rather forward-thinking. It helped that she'd been a constable with the Met and that he was a father of four daughters, who likely made it clear that they wanted what they wanted despite their gender.

Miguel handed Rosa the keys to his car. "Mamá will kill me if I leave early. No need for both of us to suffer."

"How will you get home?" Rosa asked.

"Sanchez or one of my brothers. I'll walk you out."

After a long goodbye, Rosa started the ignition. She was just about to pull away when through her open window, she heard a female voice with a distinct Spanish accent coming from the end of the street just near the intersection.

"I don't care!"

A familiar baritone voice responded, "You'll care if I tell you to!"

Two people, silhouetted by the lamppost, stood on the sidewalk. Rosa couldn't make out the woman's features in the dark except that she was of slim build. However, Salvador Vasquez's low voice confirmed his presence. The red ember of his cigarette drew up-and-down lines in the dark as he moved his arms. His voice was too quiet to hear what he was saying, but it was clear he was trying to placate the young lady.

"I do not care." The woman stormed away, shouting as she left, "Not only that, you owe me!"

The investigator in Rosa caused her curiosity to be heightened, but her practicality reminded her that Mr. Vasquez's problems were none of her business.

As she drove away, she saw a man in his early thirties sitting in a parked black Ford. He had slicked-back, black hair in a pompadour, like so many younger men did. A long scar marred a broad, attractive face.

He tipped his hat as Rosa passed by, and she pretended not to see him. She was about two blocks away when the sound of fireworks could be heard in the distance, and she now wished she'd stayed to watch.

7

*T*he next morning, Rosa stood by the window in the second-floor office of Rosa Reed Investigations and stared down at Santa Bonita's business district. Diego sat on the windowsill and, with a limber hind leg, scratched at his ear. He seemed to be in a certain wistful mood as he posed on the sill, taking in the activity below. Rosa hummed along to Billy Williams' song, "I'm Gonna Sit Right Down and Write Myself a Letter," playing on the radio.

She'd been excited to open her office the year before, enlisting Gloria's help to make it into a comfortable yet efficient workspace with a sitting area, a desk, bookshelf, kitchenette, and a large closet she'd converted to a darkroom. Rosa was always eager to arrive in the morning, make some coffee, and phone the messenger service that handled her calls.

The coffee percolator gurgled loudly, announcing it was ready to serve. Rosa poured herself a cup, musing over the vibrant party from the day before. She idly wondered if there was a term for it, the sudden and disorientating immersion into a different expression of life than one was used to. Almost like a cultural jolt, or a shock, one might say.

This was her new extended family. She shook her head slowly, thinking about it as she blew on her hot coffee. There was some underlying tension, even beyond the demand and expectation for a second wedding, but all families had their share of that. The Belmontes were opinionated by nature and were bound to butt heads occasionally.

It was fine. They were fine. She was going to have a wonderful, colorful—and judging from last night—loud life with them.

Rosa lifted her fingers to admire her ring, a symbol that the Belmontes had surprisingly missed the night before—dim light and cerveza to be thanked for that.

She waved it at Diego, who answered the gesture with a bored yawn. "No regrets this time."

Having narrowly escaped a bad engagement, Rosa would never forget her dear friend Lady Vivien Eveleigh and was relieved that her murder had been solved. Vivien's death and Rosa's inability to solve the crime had been the primary driving forces of her investigative career so far. Rosa excelled in her police training and had proven to be a formidable constable and an effective sleuth. Her aptitude had obviously been inherited from her parents. Her father, now retired Superintendent Basil Reed of Scotland Yard, was a well-respected leader in the police community in London. Her mother, Ginger Reed, otherwise known as Lady Gold, was a renowned private investigator.

Rosa's pedigree was clear. But pedigree is one thing; undeniable passion and focus are quite another. Rosa had always wanted to follow in her parents' footsteps, but not until Vivien's murder had it become her singular obsession.

Diego meowed, jumped onto the terra-cotta-tiled floor, stretched lazily, and then slowly meandered to Rosa's desk. He stared up at the top for a moment before gathering himself and then quickly jumping onto it. After prancing delicately around the "In-Out" trays and unopened mail, he got to the black telephone, sat on his haunches, and swished his tail back and forth.

At that moment, the telephone rang.

"How did you know?" Rosa asked Diego, incredulous.

Despite the abruptness of the sound, Diego didn't flinch or startle. He stared at Rosa as if he'd been expecting the call.

"Silly cat." Rosa picked up the receiver.

"Rosa Reed Investigations."

"Hiya. No Gloria today?"

Gloria helped Rosa with office duties occasionally when she was in between career pursuits.

"Hi, Miguel, love. I'm afraid you'll have to settle for me."

"You're the only one I want to settle with, *mi belleza*. I'm counting the days!"

Rosa smiled into the receiver. "Oh, you're so sweet."

"Glad you think so, but I'm not calling to be amorous."

"Oh?"

"Can you meet me at my mother's house?"

Rosa stiffened. Mrs. Belmonte was legally her mother-in-law, but she was a strong personality, and

Rosa felt like she'd had enough of her for a while. She couldn't say that, though. "Certainly, but why?"

"Bring your 'crime-busting kit.'" Miguel had used a cute term to describe the things Rosa usually carried around with her, like lockpicks, notepad, her camera, and sometimes even a handgun. He had often joked about it, but this time his voice was somber.

"I don't understand. Is your mom all right?"

"Yes, she's okay . . . but she's very upset." Miguel sighed heavily. "There's been a murder. Would you like to consult?"

"I'll be right there."

8

*R*osa parked her Corvette adjacent to a police cruiser and hurried past the small grove of mature oak trees in a large unoccupied residential lot just off the street.

Near the T-intersection of Camino Coronado and Hornby Street, just around the corner but hidden by the trees from where she had seen Salvador Vasquez as they left the party, two more police cruisers created a barrier. More officers kept the small crowd at bay, having roped off the area.

Carrying her "crime kit," Rosa nodded at one of the police officers who knew her, ducked under the rope, and walked toward what looked like a fairly new red-and-white Ford Sunliner convertible. The car was parked with nose, bug-eyed headlights, and narrow chrome grille pointed away from Rosa.

Miguel and Detective Sanchez were there, along with Officer Richardson, a surly middle-aged police photographer busy snapping photographs. Chief Medical Examiner Melvyn Philpott leaned in the open passenger door, wearing his fedora and black-rimmed glasses. He moved with slow deliberation as he straightened up, unable to suppress the accompanying groan, and removed his black-framed glasses, which he attempted to clean with his thin black tie. He said something to Detective Sanchez, who scribbled on a notepad.

Miguel looked up and waved Rosa over.

"Mrs. Belmonte."

Rosa cocked her head and looked out from under her eyelashes. "That would be Miss Reed—"

"To everyone else. To me, you're Mrs. Belmonte."

If it weren't for the shocked gazes of the constables seeing this uncharacteristic display of affection, Rosa would've happily continued with their playful banter. But she stepped away from her husband, out of arm's reach for good measure, smoothed her full skirt, and cleared her throat. "What do we have here?"

The crime victim was slumped over on the car's

front seat with his head hanging over the edge on the passenger side.

Rosa wrinkled her nose. "Salvador Vasquez?"

Miguel answered stiffly, "Yup."

Wearing the same clothes from the night before —western-style shirt fastened with a bolo tie—Mr. Vasquez had a bloodied bullet hole in his temple, with dried blood covering the left side of his face. The white-leather bench seat and the inside of the passenger door were splattered as well.

"Hello, Miss Reed," Dr. Philpott said.

"Dr. Philpott," Rosa returned. "How's Mrs. Philpott?"

"She's good. Busy with her rose garden."

"How nice for her." Rosa turned her attention back to Miguel and the body in the car. "Time of death, Dr. Philpott?"

"The body is still in rigor mortis but loosening," Dr. Philpott said. "I'd say eight to twelve hours ago. Probably happened mid to late evening."

"No one heard a gun go off," Detective Sanchez said. "Officers canvassing the neighborhood have come up blank."

Rosa shared a look with Miguel. "The fireworks? They'd work with Dr. Philpott's estimated time of death."

"It would make a good cover," Miguel said. "It also means the execution was timed."

Rosa nodded. "And that the killer was aware of the birthday party."

"Carlotta and I were still at the party when the fireworks went off," Detective Sanchez said. "We didn't notice a gun going off, and naturally, no one else did either. It was pretty much bedlam at the party by the time the firecrackers went off."

"It's clear the killer approached the car from the driver's side and fired at fairly close range," Miguel said.

"But not too close," Dr. Philpott said. "No sign of gunpowder residue on the body. I would say it could have been just about where Detective Sanchez is standing right now." He closed his black medical bag. "I'm off to the morgue. Will the body be released to me soon?"

Miguel nodded. "The ambulance is on standby."

"Very good." Dr. Philpott tipped his hat. "Good day."

Rosa waved as the pathologist got in his car and drove away, then turned back to the crime scene in front of her.

"There is no sign of a bullet hitting the inside of the passenger door," Rosa said, looking closely. "It must have passed through the open window." She scouted the area and gestured. "The killer could've hidden behind one of those oak trees and then stepped forward just as Mr. Vasquez got in behind the driver's wheel." She caught Miguel's eye. "Are there footprints?"

Miguel shook his head. "Already looked. The ground is too hard around the car, and there's grass under the trees." He pointed to the large weed-filled adjacent lot. "The bullet is somewhere there. I'll get some guys to search it."

"When was the body found and by whom?" Rosa asked.

"Nine this morning by a passerby," Miguel said. "He was on his way to the bus stop on the far corner there to catch his shift at the lumberyard. He rushed home and phoned it in when he saw the body. He said the only reason he noticed it is because he walked over here to admire the car."

Rosa pursed her lips, then asked, "What about Francisca?"

"She'd parked her car way down at the end near where we were parked," Miguel said. "She probably drove off in the opposite direction."

"I saw him leave the party," Rosa said. "Francisca knew that he'd left already too. I can only guess why, but surely she must have noticed that he didn't come home?"

"I want to give her some time to deal with her grief," Miguel said, "but unfortunately, I can't wait too long before asking her questions."

"A young woman was arguing with Salvador just as I was leaving." Rosa motioned to the general area. "Unfortunately, I didn't see her very well, but she was upset about something."

"Hmm," Miguel muttered. "Whoever it was, she herself was probably the last person to see him alive. We need to find out who that was."

Rosa contemplated the fact that she herself was also among the last to see Salvador Vasquez alive.

"There's something else," she said. "I saw a man in a black Ford sedan just across from where we were parked—like he was waiting for someone."

Detective Sanchez snorted. "That sounds suspicious, all right."

"Whoever he is, he is now definitely a suspect," Miguel offered.

"Unfortunately, I didn't get a good look at him," Rosa said.

"There are no other witnesses as yet," Detective Sanchez said, "but we haven't really started going through the list of party attendees Mrs. Belmonte provided."

Miguel looked downcast as he stared at his mother's house. "This includes most of my family members. I'm afraid this investigation is going to become a conflict of interest for me." He gave Rosa a meaningful look. "Which is why I asked you to help."

Rosa stepped away from the Sunliner and the small group gathered there. Reaching into her bag, she removed her Argus 35 mm camera and took pictures of the general area, starting with the dirt-covered entrance to the lot just off Camino Coronado. As she continued down the street, she captured different angles of the lot, then moved back to the car where she snapped the interior, body included.

Letting her camera hang on the straps wrapped around her neck, Rosa clasped her fingers together and pointed a finger as if shooting a gun at the car driver. She concluded that if the shooter were as tall or taller than she was, the bullet would have gone straight through the skull without changing direction too much. It would have followed a downward trajectory through the victim's skull, then out the open window. The chances of finding any signs of a rico-chet mark in the dirt were very slim, but she headed to that area and searched anyway. She found nothing.

A small cropping of trees lay just beyond, and Rosa searched the trunks, but again, came up empty. She gazed over at the distant house bordering the lot at the back. Rosa would have to let the police search there, although she doubted the bullet would have gone that far, unless it had been discharged from a high-powered rifle.

She stepped into the back alley, noting a gate that led to Mrs. Belmonte's backyard. By the look of its rusted hinges and the wild vines obscuring it, the gate seemed neglected and rarely used. Rosa tested the latch. The creaking of the joints sounded loud in the quiet of the day but would easily have been drowned out by the boisterous party music. An empty lot next door gave easy access to the street. *Anyone* from the party could've snuck out, stolen across the empty lot, shot Salvador Vasquez, and then returned without being missed.

"I have already covered this whole scene."

Rosa jerked toward the voice of Officer Richard-son. In his midforties, the officer was rather dour-looking, with big, droopy eyelids and a crooked nose that looked as if it had been broken at least one time.

He had a bit of a middle-aged paunch, bulging out slightly from above his leather belt. His police uniform was always ironed and starched, but it didn't serve to make his appearance any smarter-looking.

Richardson scowled as Rosa returned to the scene, camera in hand. He and Rosa had gotten off on the wrong foot—the only thing Rosa could attribute this to was that she was female and foreign. She countered his frown with a smile. "It doesn't hurt to have more."

"Yeah, well, you have to know where to point the lens," Officer Richardson said. Opening his large leather camera bag, he unscrewed his camera lens and started putting away his equipment. "I have training for that, you know. And the shots have to be properly developed."

The agitated tone of voice made it clear that Richardson didn't like Rosa intruding on his territory. And he wasn't going to like what she was about to say next.

"Officer Richardson, I have been officially asked to join in on this case, just as I have in previous cases. I can assure you I know how to handle a camera, and I have my own darkroom."

Slinging his camera bag over his shoulder, he

said, "You're only here because you're in Belmonte's pocket. You know it, and I know it."

Rosa bristled. "I assure you, I'm here on my own merits. Have you forgotten that I was a constable in London?"

He snorted derisively. "So why didn't you stay there, then?"

Rosa stared, jaw slack, at the rude man as he strolled to one of the police cruisers.

Shaking off the contempt—it wasn't the first time she'd been judged for her job and unconventional placement in society, and it wouldn't be the last—Rosa took more photographs. She walked to the nearest fence lining the backyard of the first house. Finding a mound of dirt near the back of the property, she climbed on top to look at the backyards and the alley servicing the houses on the street. There were a few more undeveloped lots dotted with tall grass, oak, and eucalyptus. Rosa walked down the alley taking pictures until she reached Maria Belmonte's house, where she snapped a few more and then headed back to the crime scene.

By the time she got there, an ambulance was driving away with the body, and the police were dispersing.

Miguel approached her. "I've asked Sanchez to

return to the station and fill Delvecchio in on what we've found so far. I'd like to see my mom now and speak to Francisca."

"Do you want me to join you?"

Miguel nodded, and Rosa joined him on the sidewalk. For the second time in less than twelve hours, Rosa and Miguel walked up the stone pathway to the front door of Maria Belmonte's house. There was no loud music today and no children to be seen. Rosa could hear Miguel take a deep breath before he knocked on the door lightly. Without waiting for an answer, he turned the knob and walked in.

9

*M*rs. Belmonte, her tan face tense, deepening her wrinkles, sat beside Miguel's Aunt Francisca on the couch—a Spanish design with leather seat cushions and a base made of woven strips of thin wood—in the living room. A pot of coffee and two cups sat on a small table in front of them. The distraught, newly widowed woman clutched a tissue, dabbing at red, puffy eyes.

Miguel's mother waved them over, and Rosa sat on one of the matching chairs and offered her condolences. "My deepest sympathies to you both," she said. Then, she inconspicuously took out her notepad.

Miguel dragged the other chair closer to the table

and leaned forward. "Again, I'm so sorry, Tía Francisca."

Mrs. Vasquez stared with red-rimmed eyes. "I've almost run out of tears."

Mrs. Belmonte patted the distressed woman's hand as she protested. "He was a good man! Why would anyone want to kill him?"

"I don't know, Mamá, but we are going to find out," Miguel said. Of his aunt, he asked, "Do you think you can answer a few questions now?"

After a moment's hesitation, Mrs. Vasquez nodded.

"You might remember me mentioning that Rosa has helped us a lot on past investigations," Miguel continued. "I've asked her to help on this one as well."

"Of course," his aunt said weakly.

"I understand how shocking the sudden death of a loved one can be," Rosa said.

Mrs. Vasquez lowered her gaze. "You've lost someone?"

Rosa nodded. "My dearest friend. Now, would you mind if I asked you a few questions?"

Miguel nodded to his aunt in encouragement, and when the lady returned the gesture, Rosa began.

"How did you and Mr. Vasquez meet?" Starting

with a question out of reference sometimes helped to calm the person, especially if it made them think of something happier.

"It was simple and romantic," Mrs. Vasquez replied. "At the time, I worked at a bookstore not far from here. He came in one day to buy a book." She managed a weak smile. "He never did buy anything, and later he said that once he laid eyes on me, thoughts of reading flew from his mind."

Rosa nodded, encouraging Mrs. Vasquez to continue.

"Salvador was straightforward. You always knew what he was thinking. And so handsome! From the moment the little bell rang above the door, I couldn't take my eyes off him. He must've noticed me staring. A short while later, he asked me out to dinner. I hadn't been on a date in many, many years, but by the time we started dessert, I was hopelessly in love. I felt like a schoolgirl at forty-nine years old!"

Rosa smiled. "And he must have fallen for you quickly too!"

"Yes, he did! We had much in common. I was a widow, and he was a widower. His wife died over ten years ago in Mexico. I know it sounds strange, but we only dated for two months before he proposed. We were married soon after." Mrs.

Vasquez looked to Mrs. Belmonte, who nodded back in support, and then let out a long sigh. "Miguel, as you might know, my first husband died when we were only twenty. We never had a chance to have children. I was single for a long time and never thought I would marry again."

"What time did you leave the party last night, Tía Francisca?" Miguel asked.

"I . . . I don't really remember exactly."

"She left at ten thirty-five, Miguel," Mrs. Belmonte said. "Salvador left much earlier—around eight last night, without saying goodbye. A man I didn't recognize came to get him. He probably just walked in, as no one would have heard the doorbell."

"I saw him leave too," Rosa said. "I left not long after that." Turning to Mrs. Vasquez, she asked, "Did you know the man who came to fetch him?"

"His name is Simon Rennings," Mrs. Vasquez said. "He works for Salvador."

"What did Salvador say to you before he left?" Rosa asked. She inclined her head. "I saw him speaking to you."

Mrs. Vasquez's jaw tightened. "He told me that something important had come up at work and that he had to leave immediately."

"You weren't alarmed when you got home and he wasn't there?" Rosa asked.

Mrs. Vasquez squinted as she considered the question. "Yes, I was. But I just thought that whatever issue took him away was not yet resolved. I awoke in the middle of the night, and he still wasn't in. I started to worry. I called his office, but of course, there was no answer that time of night."

Rosa poised her pen over her notebook. "What is his business called?"

"MexAmera Trade Solutions," Mrs. Vasquez said. "The office is downtown, but only Mr. Rennings and a secretary work there. She's new. In fact, I met her for the first time at the party last night. Mrs. Delgado."

"She's a friend of Patricia's," Mrs. Belmonte explained.

"Hector's wife," Rosa confirmed. "Yes, I saw her last night. Is she from Mexico too?"

Mrs. Belmonte sniffed. "I can only assume. Oh, this is so upsetting! Miguel, you must find out who did this awful thing!"

"I plan to, Mamá."

"We'll do our best, Mrs. Belmonte," Rosa said kindly. "We promise."

Mrs. Belmonte's dark eyes softened. "Yes, I believe you will."

Rosa continued, "I saw a lady arguing with Salvador last night as I left. From her accent, I could tell she was Latina. It could have been Mrs. Delgado, but it was too dark to see. Would you have any idea who else that could have been?"

Mrs. Vasquez's eyes widened in surprise. "No, I have no idea."

Addressing everyone, Rosa asked, "Did any of you happen to notice if Mrs. Delgado was still at the party during the fireworks?"

Miguel thought for a moment. "I don't think I saw her there. But that's not conclusive. I just didn't notice."

Mrs. Vasquez lifted a shoulder and shook her head.

"If she left before that, she didn't tell me," Mrs. Belmonte said.

"How about afterwards?" Rosa pressed. "Did anyone notice if she was there or not?"

Mrs. Belmonte's tired eyes grew round. "I remember now. Yes, she was. She said goodbye to me about an hour after the fireworks."

"So, she could have left and come back?" Rosa asked.

"That's possible," Miguel said, "but that question will be asked of everyone at the party when Detective Sanchez interviews them. It's standard protocol in cases like this. If someone noticed her slip out, we'll find out."

Miguel turned back to his aunt. "How much do you know about Salvador's business?"

"Well, in retrospect, I wish I had asked more questions about it." Mrs. Vasquez took another tissue from the Kleenex box and blew her nose. "I do know that they consulted both import and export for companies on both sides of the Mexico and USA border."

Rosa and Miguel shared a look.

"Do you know if he specialized in any particular type of goods?" Miguel asked.

Mrs. Vasquez held Miguel's gaze. "Like clothing or food? Sure. All kinds of things."

"I'm sorry, but I have to ask this, Tía," Miguel said softly. "Could Salvador have been involved in importing illegal substances?"

"No, no," Mrs. Vasquez said sternly. "Absolutely not."

"But how do you know for sure?" Miguel said, keeping his gaze on his aunt. "You hadn't known him that long."

"I know because we talked about that," Mrs. Vasquez said. "Salvador detested the things Enrique was involved in. He told me they were a bunch of snakes."

Rosa and Miguel shared another look.

"Who's Enrique?" Miguel said.

"Oh, I'm sorry, Miguel," Mrs. Vasquez said. "Salvador has a younger brother named Enrique. He lives here in Santa Bonita." She faced Mrs. Belmonte. "Maria, you knew that, didn't you?"

Mrs. Belmonte pouted. "No, you never mentioned him before. Why have you not mentioned him before? He wasn't at your wedding."

Mrs. Vasquez stared at the mangled tissue in her hand and whispered, "He was in jail. That's why we never talked about him. That's why he wasn't at our wedding."

To Rosa and Miguel, she said, "Salvador had a lot of respect for the law and couldn't understand why his brother didn't. Salvador was very grateful to make a new start in America and was always mindful of being a good citizen. I never even saw him drive above the speed limit!"

"Do you know what kind of things Enrique was involved in specifically?" Rosa asked. "What was he jailed for?"

"Breaking and entering, I think. Enrique wasn't behind bars for that long. This time. Salvador mentioned his brother had been involved in dealing in the past."

"Dealing?" Rosa said. "As in drugs."

It was common knowledge among the international law enforcement community that a burgeoning system of importing illegal drugs, especially opium, from Mexico into America was growing in influence. Rosa had come across an article about it recently. Farmers in northwest Mexico had been growing larger amounts of opium poppies to meet the demand. Since then, it had become big business for unscrupulous characters, particularly the mafia, in New York and closer to home in Hollywood. Cocaine was also a problem.

Mrs. Vasquez nodded. "Yes, something like that. Salvador said that Enrique had always been a bad man, even in Mexico, and that he had broken his mother's heart many times and brought shame to their father."

"Are the parents still alive?" Rosa asked.

"No, they died some time ago." Mrs. Vasquez stared blankly, in thought for a moment. "You know it's so strange when two brothers carry such strong physical resemblance to one another and yet are so different."

Rosa cocked a brow. "They looked alike?"

"Oh yes. I've only seen a picture, but you could easily mistake them for identical twins. Enrique is a year younger, but the resemblance is uncanny. Salvador said Enrique has a reputation as a womanizer. My dear Salvador was a faithful man, staying true to his first wife until she died of cancer in forty-six." She dabbed at her eyes with her tissue. "And to me, of course."

"Has anyone contacted Enrique yet?" Miguel asked.

"No . . . I mean, I haven't," Mrs. Vasquez said, "so I assume he still doesn't know."

A noise from the back of the house interrupted the interview, and they all looked toward the doorway to the kitchen area. The door was open to the back porch.

Mrs. Belmonte called out, "Is someone there?"

Miguel put his hand on his sidearm and motioned for his mother to stay seated.

After a long moment, the soft sound of shuffling feet could be heard, and the frail form of Mrs. Gonzales appeared in the kitchen entryway, blinking rapidly as if waking up from a dream.

"Consuela!" Mrs. Belmonte said as she got up from the sofa and approached the confused-looking older lady, then disappeared into the kitchen. Her voice carried to the living room. "*¿De donde vienes? Can't find your own back door again?*"

"Poor thing," Rosa commented. "Does she get lost often?"

Miguel nodded. "And she's highly superstitious, as we saw last night, so she frightens easily as well."

"Actually . . ." Mrs. Vasquez started, her eyes unfocused as if she was in her own world. "I can't help but wonder if there is a curse at work."

Miguel pulled back, ducking his chin. "I don't think so."

"Why not? My brother Luis, your father, died much too early. My first husband died young. Don't forget about your cousin Orlando who died just last year. And your grandfather's brother, Guillermo, he—"

"He immigrated to the United States with his parents," Miguel said, finishing for her. "And was killed in the Great War like millions of others. Look, Tía Francisca, it's normal for a family of this size to have a few deaths occur. It doesn't mean Mexican witchcraft is at play. In fact, as tragic as they all are, it would be strange if there were no deaths. The world has come through two world wars in less than forty-five years."

"My mother lost her first husband in the First World War," Rosa offered. "And there are early deaths in my family tree as well, both men and women."

"I . . . I suppose you're right," Mrs. Vasquez said.

Rosa had seen this before, especially with a woman twice widowed. The mind struggles to find a reason for the heartache, sometimes reaching for superstition as an answer. Her heart went out to Miguel's aunt.

"I think we're done for now," Miguel said kindly. "If you think of anything else, Tía, please let me know." He called to his mother in the kitchen. "Are you all right in there?"

"Si, si. Consuela is just having some cake left over from last night. I'll take her home later. Don't forget about your meeting with Father Navarro!"

10

*S*t. Francis Church sat on a corner lot near the center of Santa Bonita. The attractive edifice had a white-stucco exterior with Spanish-style arches and a bell tower and was accented with deep-green fronds of palm-tree clusters. Rosa was familiar with the Catholic Church from her time as a police constable in London when certain investigations required a chat with someone at the local church. Still, she had never given the institution much consideration until now.

They were greeted by a kindly, talkative nun, dressed in a black habit adorned with a necklace with a single large wooden cross hanging from it. Her wimple framed a face covered with laugh lines. "I'm Sister Evangeline. Is that you, Mr. Belmonte?

You've changed since I saw you last. Handsomer! And you must be Miss Reed. We're so pleased to see you here at St. Francis."

"Sister Evangeline oversees the Holy Mother's Hand of Hope," Miguel said as they followed the nun. "It's a charity to assist girls in need."

"We're all God's creatures," Sister Evangeline chirped, "every one of us, no matter our circumstances."

When they reached the priest's office, Sister Evangeline took Rosa's hand. "I do hope we'll see you again soon. Both of you."

Father Navarro, soft in the face and with a slight belly paunch visible under his cassock, had kind eyes with wrinkles befitting a man in his fifties. He welcomed Miguel and greeted Rosa with the same warmth as Sister Evangeline, then directed them to sit in chairs already arranged in a small circle. His office at St. Francis Church was humble, with simple furnishings consisting of a desk, a stack of chairs, and a set of shelves filled with books.

Father Navarro smiled, flashed large white teeth, and said, "Mr. Belmonte, your mother, Maria, is a valued member of our parish. As you're aware, she has recently visited me." His eyes landed on Rosa. "She's in a considerable amount of distress. She's made it very clear that she intends for all her children to marry in the Catholic Church."

"Yes," Rosa said, holding the priest's gaze. "She's already given us a date."

Father Navarro worked his lips. "About that, I'm afraid a month may be a little ambitious."

"Why is that?" Miguel asked. "Whatever it takes, I'm sure my mother will arrange it. Invitations, reception, flowers . . ."

"It's not the particulars of the ceremony that are in question, Mr. Belmonte," Father Navarro said, "but the laws of the Church. Laws that go back years and which I have no power to change."

Had Rosa been wearing pearls, she would be clutching them right now. "What do you mean?"

"Baptized Catholics," he glanced at Miguel, "such as Mr. Belmonte, and baptized non-Catholics—" His gaze returned to Rosa. "I presume you've been baptized as an Episcopalian?"

"Church of England," Rosa answered.

Father Navarro continued, "Yes, well, a union between the two of you cannot happen unless a bishop permits it."

With a note of annoyance, Miguel said, "Okay, how do we do that?"

"I'll have to write a letter pleading your case, and

then we wait," Father Navarro returned.

Miguel's eyes flashed with the concern Rosa felt. He asked, "For how long?"

Father Navarro lifted a shoulder, his lips pinched as he extended a look of apology. "It's anyone's guess. The bishop is a busy man."

"Can't you plead our case as urgent?" Miguel pressed.

"I'll do my best, but you must accept that there is a possibility that he'll say no," Father Navarro said.

Alarmed, Rosa asked, "Why wouldn't the bishop give his permission?"

"Our archbishop is a very conservative man," Father Navarro said. "He simply might not agree to it."

He took a sip of water from a glass that sat on his desk. "Forgive me; I should've asked if you'd like a drink. One of the sisters can get you something. Water? Coffee or Tea?"

"We're fine," Rosa said, answering for them both. Her eagerness to get to the bottom of the matter was the only thing of importance at the moment. "Are you saying we can't get married?"

Father Navarro smiled softly. "It's my under-standing that you are already married."

"We are," Miguel said, "but do you consider us

married?"

"Certainly, your union is legal."

"Father Navarro," Rosa started, feeling rather worn out by the circular nature of this conversation. "What is it that you propose we do? How do we make Mrs. Belmonte happy?"

"I'm afraid she won't be happy without a mass, which, as a non-Catholic, Miss Reed—it's all right if I call you Miss Reed? Mrs. Belmonte feels rather off point."

"Miss Reed is fine," Rosa said.

"Yes, as I was saying, Miss Reed," Father Navarro continued, "you wouldn't be permitted to take communion, nor, clearly, would any of your family members."

"I'm not taking communion at my wedding if my wife isn't taking it," Miguel said.

"It's not necessary," Father Navarro said. "It's perfectly acceptable to enter the sacrament of marriage without the mass being part of the ceremony." After a soft sigh, he added, "But your mother won't be happy about that."

"Let me deal with my mother," Miguel said with a note of defiance.

"Yes, of course," Father Navarro said. "There is also another matter you must consider. To be married in the Catholic Church, you will have to promise to raise any children that may come from this union in the Catholic faith."

Miguel bit his lip as he stared at Rosa. She gave him a gentle nod. They hadn't discussed how they'd raise their children, but in her mind, if they loved them unconditionally, like God himself did, they would find their own way.

"We promise," Miguel said. He turned back to Father Navarro. "Are you sure this will work?"

"As long as we hear back from the bishop."

Miguel chuckled dryly. "Father Navarro, this ceremony will take place regardless, and my mother will be delighted if none-the-wiser."

"Mr. Belmonte," Father Navarro began, "it's not in my nature to practice deception, but, in this case, I'm willing to turn a blind eye."

Miguel jumped to his feet and extended his hand. "Deal."

Father Navarro shook Miguel's hand, then extended one to Rosa. "Do you find this arrangement suitable, Miss Reed?"

"I do," Rosa said, then laughed. "I wonder how many times I'll have to say that?"

Miguel wrapped an arm around her shoulders. "At least one more time."

11

*A*fter saying goodbye to Miguel, who had to return to the precinct—and after many reassurances—Rosa headed back to her office. Usually, she kept the small kitchen in her office stocked with enough food for a light lunch, but she hadn't had time to shop since her return from England.

Besides, after the meeting they'd just had with Father Navarro, Rosa found her stomach was too topsy-turvy to eat. Mrs. Belmonte was so set on all her children being married in the Catholic Church—which in her mind, included the liturgy of the mass—and as Miguel's mother, she wielded a lot of power. Rosa had seen her share of domestic disturbances and knew it took only one family member to make life miserable for everyone.

What if the bishop didn't respond in time or, worse, forbade the wedding? Miguel was determined to go through with a ceremony of any kind, legitimate or not, to appease his mother. And what if Mrs. Belmonte discovered the truth about that? Rosa let out a long, slow breath. She would be cast out of the Belmonte family for sure.

With her mind on this very personal dilemma, Rosa was surprised to find she hadn't driven to the office, but rather, she was back at the crime scene. One's subconscious shouldn't be ignored.

It had been over three hours since the police had arrived, and the body had been taken away. The tow truck was there to take the car into evidence, with one officer left to monitor the driver.

Rosa parked across from the empty lot, but when she stepped out of her Corvette, she felt a drop of rain hit her hand. Ominous dark clouds had formed over the last hour and rolled over the tall trees. She reached behind the back seat's armrest for the button to release the rear compartment lid where the canvas top was stored. She took a few minutes to extend the cover over to the windshield and wrestle with snap mechanisms to hold the cover in place. By the time she had finished with the cover and rolled up the windows, the rain was coming down hard. She hopped back into the car just in time to watch the tow truck round the corner towing Salvador Vasquez's Ford Sunliner, the lone police officer following in his cruiser. She watched as they turned onto the cross street and disappeared. The scene of the crime was now empty.

She sat for a moment, debating whether to dig out her umbrella—a necessary accessory in London, but a novelty in California used in rare cases of rain-storms like this one—or to just come back later. The rain would probably erase any clues that might still be there anyway.

The increasingly loud sound of rain drumming on the Corvette's top helped her decide. Just as Rosa was about to put the car into gear, an all-black Cadillac Eldorado came from her rear, slowed, and turned the corner. The rain obscured her vision, and by the time she had her windshield wipers going, she'd missed her chance to view the driver. The car parked just a few feet away from the spot where the Sunliner had been.

The driver looked her way, and Rosa gasped. If she didn't know better, she'd swear she was staring at Salvador Vasquez! He had the same handsome profile—his black sideburns poking out from under a cowboy hat—and could easily have been the man Rosa had just seen earlier that morning covered in blood and lying dead on his car seat.

"Enrique," Rosa muttered.

It was as if Salvador had been strangely resurrected, returning to the site of his own murder. With shoulders sagging, he drew his hand up to cover his mouth and face. Was he weeping?

Rosa started her engine, then pulled up beside the Cadillac while the driver watched her in surprise.

With the car idling, she rolled down her window. He did the same.

"Enrique Vasquez?" Rosa asked.

"Who are you?" His Spanish accent was strong, like his brother's.

"My name is Rosa Reed. I'm a private investigator working as a special consultant to the Santa Bonita Police Department."

"You're the British woman that is seeing one of the Belmonte boys."

"Yes, that's right. Condolences on the loss of your brother."

He turned and stared straight ahead again, his expression distant.

"Do you mind if I ask you a few questions now while we're both here?" Rosa turned off her ignition. As it was known to do, the weather in California suddenly shifted, rain clouds thinning, making room for thin rays of sun. She opened her car door and stepped outside.

As Enrique Vasquez scowled at her request, Rosa hurried to add, "You might shed light on who would want to hurt your brother. You do want to help catch his killer, don't you?"

"*Si*, of course." His door opened, and he stepped out wearing jeans and a white shirt, and a pair of snakeskin cowboy boots. Closing the door, he leaned against it.

"How did you find out your brother had died?" Rosa asked.

"A friend who lives in the neighborhood recognized Salvador's Sunliner and saw the cops here. He called me. I parked down the street and watched. I saw them take his body away. It was pretty obvious he was dead."

"What is the name of your friend?"

Enrique stared as if surprised by the question. "It doesn't matter. He wouldn't appreciate me dropping his name, if you know what I mean."

It seemed to be an unlikely coincidence that a

friend happened to live on the same street; however, Enrique Vasquez was sincerely grieved at the sudden loss of his brother, and if Rosa pushed too hard, he might become uncooperative.

"He died as the result of a gunshot," Rosa said softly. "Do you have any idea who might have done such a thing?"

"No. Nobody." Enrique's jaw clenched. "My brother was a stand-up guy."

"That's what his wife says too."

"Everyone who knew him would say the same. I . . . I was always the one in trouble. When we were kids growing up in San Felipe, he was always the one who pulled me out of the messes I got myself into."

"According to Mrs. Vasquez, you and Salvador didn't see eye to eye."

"We've barely spoken in two years." He slapped the roof of his car. "*¡Dios mío!* Why didn't I reach out more?" He pinched his nose as if that would eliminate his pain. "He was so stubborn."

"You obviously still cared for your brother, whatever the differences you had, and I'm sure he felt the same way," Rosa said kindly. "What was it exactly that kept you apart?" When he didn't respond, she decided to press just a bit. "Mr. Vasquez, it's a murder investigation. Anything could be . . ."

"Let's just say he didn't approve of some of the people I associate with."

"Why is that?"

When Enrique failed to respond, Rosa changed her tactic. "Would any of those people have something against him?"

"He had absolutely nothing to do with them or my line of work. Like I said, he was a stand-up guy. He didn't get himself involved in . . ." He paused as if looking for the right wording. "Alternative ways to make a living."

"That's a very cryptic way to describe a career," Rosa said. "Can you be a little more forthcoming?"

"I fill a demand. I help supply certain niche markets. Sometimes it involves bending the rules a bit. Not me, of course, I don't . . . but some do." He caught her gaze. "That's all I'm going to say about my line of work, Miss Reed."

"Mr. Vasquez, I have to ask, what you were doing last night between the hours of eight p.m. and ten p.m.?"

He flashed an annoyed look. "I was at the garage. I have a car that happens to look a lot like Salvador's Sunliner. Same color, but three years older. Mine, unfortunately, has some carburetor issues. I was stuck at home. My car was in the garage."

Rosa arched a brow. "You have the same car as your brother?"

"Didn't plan it that way, but we always did have similar taste in cars. He bought his new; I bought mine used." He took out a cigarette, lit it, and inhaled deeply before blowing out a long wisp of smoke. "I didn't kill my brother, Miss Reed," he added. "No matter our differences. As they say, blood is thicker than water."

"Your brother was seen arguing with a woman here on the street just after he left the party. No description is available, just that the woman was furious. She had a slight Spanish accent. Any idea who that might have been?"

Enrique shook his head. "No idea." Opening his car door, he slid back inside, indicating that their conversation was nearing its end.

Rosa added hurriedly, "How about you, Mr. Vasquez?"

"Huh, what do you mean?" He held his cigarette out of the window and tapped the ashes off. "I already told you I didn't kill him."

"You have an identical car; you're a doppelgänger of your brother. By your own admission, you have working relationships with some . . . shall we say, *dubious* characters. Someone could have followed what they thought was your car last night. Would anyone want *you* dead, Mr. Vasquez?"

Enrique's expression darkened. "Adios, Miss Reed."

He dropped his cigarette out of the window and rolled it closed. Slamming the Cadillac into gear, he stomped on the gas as the tires spit dirt in protest.

12

Rosa considered following Enrique Vasquez, but he would probably spot her since he had just talked to her and knew she drove a white Corvette. It wouldn't do to have him lead her on a wild goose chase and get even more defensive and apprehensive during future questioning.

Instead, she would find Miguel and let him know about the encounter. The best course of action might be to place an officer in a car to "put a tail on him," as she had heard it being phrased in a recent episode of *Dragnet*.

Rosa decided to swing by her office to check for messages and perhaps make herself a sandwich.

However, the route took her past a block of businesses, and she caught sight of a bright sign that read, "MexAmera Trade Solutions."

Rosa pulled over for a quick look. After parking her car, she approached the building and studied the directory mounted on the wall beside the entrance. She found the company's office number, made her way down the carpeted hallway, and knocked.

When there was no response, Rosa tried the door handle. Finding it unlocked, she poked her head in the door. "Hello?" she called out. "Anyone here?"

The office was nicely decorated with modern furniture and wood-veneer wall paneling. On the wall was a bright poster showing Mexican-made furniture and next to it, a poster with an image of machinery in a lemon grove. An advertisement for fruit growers' equipment—clients of Salvador Vasquez, Rosa presumed. Catalogs were piled on an empty desk. There appeared to be two office doors down a hallway to the left.

"Hello?" she called again.

"Oh, hello." The man Rosa had seen briefly at the party the night before stepped through one of the doorways. He wore the same poorly fitted black suit. "I'm sorry," he continued, "the office is closed. I'm afraid there's been a . . . uh, family emergency."

"I hate to intrude," Rosa said. "I'm Miss Reed, a private investigator consulting with the police. Are you Mr. Rennings?"

"Yes, that's right." The man's deep-set eyes regarded Rosa with a look of thinly veiled suspicion.

"Detective Miguel Belmonte has solicited my help to investigate the death of your business partner, Salvador Vasquez."

"Ah, yes," Mr. Rennings mumbled. He ran his trembling hand over his balding head. "Terrible news. So unexpected. I still can't believe it. They told me you might come by here, but I thought you'd be with an officer, someone actually from the department."

Rosa was not unused to similar reactions of distrust and disrespect, particularly from men. They found it hard to understand why or how a woman could have anything to do with law enforcement or criminology.

"I assure you, Mr. Rennings, I have the full endorsement of the chief of police. Anything we discuss will be passed on to the appropriate detectives. I have consulted on several murder investigations already and have a background in police work in London."

"I just don't want to have to repeat myself when the real cops come."

"This is a murder investigation, Mr. Rennings. Don't be surprised if you have to answer the same question multiple times."

"Of course. I will be glad to cooperate in any way I can." He gestured to one of the upholstered chairs in the small reception room. "We need to get to the bottom of this awful business."

"Are you the only one here today?" Rosa took a seat.

"Yes. We have a secretary, but she only comes in on Mondays, Thursdays, and a half day on Fridays."

Rosa made a note, then said, "You were one of the last people to see Mr. Vasquez alive, Mr. Rennings."

"Really?" He blinked rapidly. "I didn't know that."

"Yes, we'll get to that in a minute," Rosa said. "But I want to get some background information first, if you don't mind."

"Certainly."

"Were you and Mr. Salvador Vasquez good friends?"

Mr. Rennings took a deep breath. "Well . . . no, I wouldn't say that. I was hired just eight months ago. I have a background in importing electrical equipment from Mexico. I answered his ad in a trade magazine and moved here from San Diego."

"And how would you say your working relationship had been going?"

"Quite well, I think. Business continues to grow as Mexico increases its exports of machinery, medical equipment, and agricultural products to the USA."

"So, you got along well?"

"Well enough. Mr. Vasquez was a persuasive man, a good negotiator in business, and quite popular with . . . well, he was generally well liked by everyone he met."

Rosa detected a hesitancy there and pressed it a bit. "Do you know of any past relationships Mr. Vasquez had with anyone who might have been holding a grudge? A former client, perhaps?"

"No. Mr. Vasquez prided himself on keeping good relationships with both current and past clients. That's one of the reasons his business grew."

"Past romances, perhaps? He and his wife had only been married a few months."

"He dated a few women before Francisca, but, uh . . . we never talked about that kind of thing."

Rosa angled her head in question. "You sound a bit hesitant."

"Well, I'm not the one to ask about that part of his life." He grimaced with distaste as he continued. "Mr. Vasquez was a smooth talker, and you could say the ladies liked him."

Rosa idly tapped her pencil eraser head on the notepad. "I saw you at the birthday party last night."

"You were there?"

"I was. My fiancé is part of the Belmonte family."

"I see."

"You came to summon Mr. Vasquez, and he left immediately afterwards. What was the issue?"

Mr. Rennings sniffed, then continued, although he seemed reluctant. "A client from Mexico City, who owns several large cattle farms, was having problems dealing with an importer in Florida. Darn beef regulatory regulations. I was working late here when he called. Mr. Vasquez had let me know where he'd be that night because he anticipated this client's call."

"Late in the day for a business call, wasn't it?"

"Regular business hours don't mean much when it comes to some of these larger money figures, Miss Reed. Anyway, I can provide you with the name and number of the client if you want to verify my story. But if you intend to call him, let me call first. I need to let him know about Mr. Vasquez's sudden passing, anyway, and brace him for a possible phone call from a police detective."

"Of course." Rosa jotted in her notebook. "Do you have any connection with the Belmonte family?"

"None."

"Do you own a gun, Mr. Rennings?"

He responded with a glare. "I really don't think I need to be answering to you, *Miss Reed.*"

Rosa was used to misogynistic treatment in her line of work. With feigned innocence, she asked, "What do you mean? It was a simple question."

"Let a policeman ask it."

"I'm here by the authority of the police, Mr. Rennings. I'll be sure to pass on that you've been uncooperative. Good day."

Mr. Rennings held up a hand. "Wait, wait! I didn't mean to offend. This whole dang affair has got my nerves twisted." He let out a blustering sigh. "I don't like guns."

"Where did you go after you left the party?"

"I went home. I got there around nine fifteen. You can ask my wife."

The word of a spouse wasn't exactly an ironclad alibi, but she'd see that an officer checked in with Mrs. Rennings just the same.

"Where did you last see Mr. Vasquez?"

"He was walking toward where I assume he had parked his car. I was double-parked in front of the Belmonte house, so I just got in my car and drove away."

"You didn't see anyone approach him? Perhaps in your rearview mirror?"

He shook his head. "I wasn't paying any attention to that."

"Did you ever meet Enrique Vasquez?"

"Who?"

"His younger brother, Enrique."

"What? No, I had no idea he even had any living family members. That's surprising."

"They were estranged," Rosa remarked.

"Hmm . . . Seems to be a lot of that going around."

"What do you mean by that?" Rosa asked.

"Nothing." Mr. Rennings shifted his weight and flicked a piece of lint off his rumpled tie. "Well . . . nothing to do with the murder case anyway."

"All the same, I'd like to know."

Annoyance flashed through his eyes, and Rosa didn't doubt he would've tossed her out by now if she hadn't been there on the authority of the Santa Bonita Police. "Our secretary, Mrs. Delgado—this really sounds like office gossip—is currently estranged from her husband, Alfonso, which is why Mr. Vasquez hired her. We normally don't hire married ladies."

"I see," Rosa said, ignoring the man's blatant bias against women. However, he was probably right, and Mrs. Delgado's marriage troubles had nothing to do with the murder.

"And now that Mr. Vasquez is gone, I'm afraid I might have to let her go. I never liked her anyway; she is a hard woman to get along with. Bad temper. Very inappropriate for a professional office."

Rosa waited. As a teenager, she had often visited her mother in her Kensington office of Lady Gold Investigations. During some of those visits, her mother would give her tips on sleuthing. It had stoked the fire in the heart of young Rosa Reed for police work. One thing Ginger Gold had taught her was how to read body language. Rosa saw the cocked eyebrow, the slight downward curve of the lips, the sideways glance, and the quick sniff through the nostrils. Mr. Rennings was eager to divulge a secret but wanted to appear reluctant to do so.

"Mrs. Delgado doesn't know that I know what she did . . ." Rennings glanced at the ceiling light and then back to Rosa.

Rosa just nodded, tapping her eraser again on the paper.

"The fact is," Rennings continued, "Mr. Vasquez caught her cheating with another man. I know she's not with her husband, but she is still married. Mr. Vasquez discussed the unpleasant situation with me but asked me not to tell anyone else. A secret is a secret, I suppose."

Rosa felt it best not to point out the irony here.

"When did he tell you this?" Rosa asked.

"Two weeks ago. He was entertaining a client at the Bayview restaurant on First Avenue. You know, at the new luxury hotel? When he arrived, he saw Mrs. Delgado leaving the restaurant with a man—not her husband. Salvador knew Mr. Delgado and would, I think, even consider him a friend, though certainly not close. The next day, Salvador confronted her in the office. How do the young people put it? Ah yes, she went 'totally ape.' Flipped her lid, you might say. Just imagine it! I don't know why Mr. Vasquez didn't fire her on the spot. The nerve!"

"Any idea who the man was that was with Mrs. Delgado?"

Mr. Rennings lifted a shoulder. "No. Mr. Vasquez said he'd never seen him before." He scowled. "She made him promise not to tell anyone. It would ruin her reputation."

The protection of one's reputation had been the motive for more than one murder. Rosa made a mental note to look up Mrs. Delgado.

13

*A*s she left the building, Rosa noticed a brand-new establishment called The Coffee Pot. It was styled after some of the coffee houses Rosa knew of in the Soho district of London, which featured old-fashioned-looking storefront marquees, usually painted in green with gold or white lettering. The billboard said one could get both a coffee and a donut for forty cents, and offered a selection of Italian and Mexican coffees from Chiapas. She wondered if Salvador Vasquez had had anything to do with the shop owner's importation of such goods.

Thinking of donuts, Rosa realized she was starving. Instead of returning to her Corvette, she turned to the coffee shop, then swiveled toward a male voice calling her.

"Good afternoon, Miss Reed. Feeling the need for a donut and coffee, are you?"

"Oh, hello, Mr. Vasquez," Rosa said with a smile. Earlier, she'd thought about following Enrique Vasquez, but perhaps he'd been following her. If so, he'd know she'd visited his brother's office.

Standing with his hands in his pockets, he cracked, "I thought Brits only drank tea."

"That's largely true," Rosa said. "But I seem to have developed a taste for coffee as well."

Enrique Vasquez gestured toward the door of the coffee shop. "After you."

Rosa nodded curtly and then, stepping inside, went straight to the counter and ordered a cup of coffee and a sugar donut.

Enrique Vasquez did the same.

Except he ordered his coffee in a wax-paper cup. By the time Rosa could ask for her mug of coffee to be poured into a paper cup, he was out of the store, and despite rushing outside, her coffee sloshing dangerously, Mr. Vasquez was long gone.

She was about to turn away when she spotted what looked like the crime scene car, a red-and-white Sunliner with Salvador Vasquez sitting at the wheel. Not a ghost, Rosa mused, but Enrique Vasquez, sipping on his coffee. She sauntered over to the passenger window and looked in. Enrique Vasquez flashed her a smile, virtually the same smile that Rosa had seen on his older brother's face at the birthday party. He reached over and rolled down the window.

Rosa asked, "Is the car running better?"

Enrique Vasquez lifted his chin. "I just picked it up from the shop. Didn't want to get my hands dirty." He held her gaze. "Get in?"

"I'm a little busy at the moment," Rosa said. There was no way in God's green earth she'd get into a vehicle with this guy. "Running errands."

"Hey, I'm sorry for being rude earlier," he said. "You caught me at a bad time."

"You were understandably upset."

Enrique Vasquez reached to turn the ignition key, but his hand stopped in midair. Then, as if he had changed his mind about something, he dropped it back down to the seat.

"Is there something you'd like to tell me?" Rosa prompted. "Something that might help your brother's case?"

"Yeah, I do. The young lady you saw arguing with Salvador on the street? I have a good idea who that might be. My brother has a daughter, Miranda Vasquez Torres. She's been trouble from the start."

14

*R*eturning to her bedroom at the Forrester mansion, Rosa reviewed her notes. She considered this new information about Salvador's daughter—did Francisca know about her? Miguel's aunt didn't mention her, but the question had never come up either.

Finding her bed irresistible, Rosa melted into her pillows, her eyes drooping shut. She knew she was in danger of a nap. Since returning from London, she hadn't had much time to rest.

Her bedroom was sizable, more so than the bedroom she would share with Miguel, and the king-size canopy bed larger as well. She'd miss the roomy built-in closet—a North American invention that hadn't made its way to Europe—and the attached bathroom. An oversized porcelain tub sat on black and white tiles. The walls were painted a soothing sea-foam green. Such a delight, soaking in bubbles after a long day of work.

Moving into Miguel's smaller home would be an adjustment, but Rosa didn't care. She loved Miguel and wanted to be with him, no matter what. She couldn't wait until she could announce her legal status as his wife, and she hoped Mrs. Belmonte appreciated the sacrifices they were making for her.

Vivien's stuffed bear, Cecil, was a new addition to Rosa's bedroom decor, and oddly, Diego had taken a liking to it. He jumped on the bed, curling up between Rosa and the bear, his purring luring her into what she appropriately termed a 'cat' nap.

When Rosa awoke, she found Diego's nose touching her cheek, his round furry body spread over her chest.

"I miss my husband," she said to her pet as she scrubbed his ears. "Shall we go for a visit?" She grabbed a small suitcase and filled it with her things. When she was done, she placed Diego in his carrying satchel.

"You must stop growing," she admonished, "or I'll not be able to carry you about for much longer."

Before she left, she scribbled a note for Gloria,

telling her not to worry if she didn't come back for the night, and slipped it under Gloria's bedroom door. Quietly, she hurried down the long staircase, not wanting to run into any family members who'd raise a brow and require an explanation.

Once in her Corvette, she roared down the long drive, the hills of Santa Bonita to her left and the sparkling Pacific Ocean to her right. Rosa felt like a rebel, as she was about to commit the misdemeanor of spending the night with her husband against her mother-in-law's wishes.

Like Miguel said when he pulled her into his arms, pushing the door of his house shut behind him with his foot. "What Mamá doesn't know won't kill her."

THEY AROSE EARLY the following day, in time to enjoy a breakfast of scrambled eggs on toast and milky coffee.

"This is nice," Rosa said.

Miguel took her hand and kissed it. "My only dream in this life, *mi amor*, is to wake up next to you every morning."

Rosa squeezed his hand. "Soon, love. We must think of your mother."

Miguel let out a frustrated breath. "*¡Madre!*" Then he smiled at Rosa. "Every sacrifice is worth it for you."

A knocking on the door caused Rosa to start. She was dressed in a lemon-colored pencil skirt with a matching short jacket, but she didn't want anyone to see her. Even an innocent delivery man could know the Belmontes and inadvertently share word of Rosa's transgression with Mrs. Belmonte.

Oh, dear. Rosa hated living a ruse and hoped Father Navarro could arrange their make-believe wedding in short order.

Miguel peered through the window before answering the door. "Sanchez," he said. "I forgot he was bringing Homer over this morning."

Detective Sanchez's warm voice boomed off the tiled ceiling. "Mornin', Belmonte. I've brought your feathered friend."

"Come in," Miguel said. "Coffee?"

"I wouldn't say no to a cup." Detective Sanchez carried a small black-leather briefcase under his arm and placed it on the coffee table in front of him. An unlit cigarette dangled from his mouth and, after removing his hat, he looked as if he had forgotten to comb his wiry black hair.

"Hello, Detective," Rosa said. When Detective

Sanchez raised a quizzical brow and shot Miguel a look, she felt her cheeks redden in embarrassment.

"Hide-e-ho," he said. Then to Miguel, "Someone had a good night."

"Hey," Miguel said sternly. "We're a married couple. Of course, you'd find Rosa here."

After hanging Homer's cage on the stand in the corner, Detective Sanchez plopped into an armchair. "By golly. My impression is that you're not married, and a wedding is being planned. Carlotta's giving me looks, too. Probably wondering when *I'm* gonna pop the question."

Miguel scowled. "I'm wondering that too. What exactly are your intentions toward my sister?"

"Hold your horses, Belmonte," Detective Sanchez said. "I've got plans. But I can't very well ask her now when you two are front and center. Would take away her spotlight."

"He has a point," Rosa said as she handed the detective a coffee heavy on cream and sugar.

Detective Sanchez pulled the dry cigarette from his lips and slid it into his shirt pocket. "Thank you." He smiled crookedly. "Don't you think you should call me Bill by now, Mrs. Belmonte?"

Rosa smiled broadly in return. "For now, I'm sticking with Miss Reed," she said, then added, "Bill."

"Oh, yes, the great ruse." Detective Sanchez guffawed. "Not many marry the same woman twice, Mick, at least not without getting divorced first."

Rosa, wanting to stop the verbal sparring before it started, quickly said, "You must call me Rosa in return, Detective."

"R-r-Rosa," Bill Sanchez said with a pronounced tongue roll. "Are you sure you're not Mexican?"

Rosa laughed. "I've got a steamship to thank for my Spanish-sounding name. I'm British through and through."

A squawk erupted from Homer's cage. "Silly cat!"

As if his tail were on fire, Diego raced through the house, over the back of the couch, then disappeared into the kitchen.

Homer screeched again, "Silly cat!"

The humans burst out laughing.

"They're certainly entertaining," Miguel said. "I wonder what would happen if I let Homer out of his cage."

"Dead bird," Detective Sanchez said dryly.

"Oh, I don't think so," Rosa returned. "I'm certain Diego's bravado would disappear, and he'd hide under the couch until Homer was locked away again."

"Shall we bring this meeting to order?" Miguel

said. He winked at Rosa. "I sounded a bit like your father there, didn't I?"

She smiled at her husband and reached for his hand. "You certainly did, *love*."

"Okay, you two," Detective Sanchez said with a snort. "No lovey-dovey before noon."

"Get on with it then," Miguel said.

Detective Sanchez straightened his tie. "We were able to get statements from everyone in the neighborhood. Nobody saw anything suspicious. The sound of the fireworks masked the gunshot."

"Clever," Rosa said. "What about the last house on that side of the block? It's the closest to where it happened. A kitchen window faces the empty lot."

"That's that old lady's house," Detective Sanchez said. "The one with the problems." He waved his finger, pointing it at his temple.

"She has a dementia illness," Miguel said with some annoyance.

"Yeah, and *that's* a problem," Detective Sanchez said testily. "Anyway, we are about halfway through interviewing everyone who was at the party, and so far, nothing. Everyone is sure all guests were there when the fireworks began."

"It doesn't necessarily mean someone couldn't have slipped away at the right moment," Miguel said.

"Not that I suspect anyone in my family. Honestly, I just want them ruled out."

"I took photographs of the back alley." Rosa faced Miguel. "There's a gate in your mom's fence that is out of view from the backyard. It leads to a shortcut to that empty lot, which gives access to Camino Coronado."

Rosa noted Miguel was frowning at the implication. Could someone in his family be a murderer? Sipping her coffee, she turned her attention back to Detective Sanchez. "Bill, have you discovered anything new?"

With a grunt, Detective Sanchez reached for the black briefcase and set it on his lap. "This was found under the front seat." Turning a brown manila envelope upside down, he produced a small, roughly made figurine of brightly colored cloth of varying thickness. He handed it to Rosa. "We've already checked for fingerprints and hair samples. Nothing."

About the size of Rosa's palm, the tied and twisted cloth fragments formed the shape of a man, with a pale piece of balled-up cloth for the head and tiny black stitching for the eyes and mouth. Instead of making the eyes round, a simple cross stitch had been used as if the figurine were dead. The hair was formed with very coarse, black thread. "A poppet doll," she said.

"I think this kind of looks like Salvador Vasquez," Detective Sanchez said. "Even has a bolo tie like the one he wears. It's not a child's toy, that's for sure. Could be *la brujería*?"

Miguel scoffed. "Mexican witchcraft?"

Detective Sanchez responded with a shrug. "Stranger things have happened."

Rosa turned the figurine over in her hand. In all her years of crime investigation, this was a first. "The power in something like this isn't derived from supernatural sources, but in the belief of the practitioner. I'll go to the library and do some research."

Miguel shifted in his seat as he set his half-empty mug of cooled coffee on the table. "*I'm* going on record saying that I don't believe my family has some curse."

"Your Aunt Francisca believes it," Rosa said gently.

"Maybe it's a Mob hit," Detective Sanchez added offhandedly. He held out the open envelope, and Rosa dropped the figurine into it.

Miguel made a face. "You think there's a *Mob* in Santa Bonita?"

"Yeah, why not?" Detective Sanchez said defensively. "It might not be Bugsy Siegel's successor, but maybe someone has set up shop here. They could have killed him by mistake."

"How does Enrique Vasquez fit in?" Miguel asked.

"He's known for shady operations," Rosa said. "I heard drugs get smuggled. Some of it ends up in Hollywood, but most of it goes to New York or Boston and places like that." She faced Detective Sanchez. "Also, it turns out Salvador Vasquez has a daughter."

"A fact he failed to mention to my aunt," Miguel said.

Detective Sanchez whistled. "Mystery kids. Never good."

"Was she the young lady I heard him arguing with?" Rosa said.

The telephone rang, and Miguel headed to the hallway to answer it.

Movement at Detective Sanchez's feet caught Rosa's eye, and before she could stop her mischievous cat, Diego attacked the detective's shoe.

He bellowed, "Hey!"

"Diego!" Rosa reached for her cat, but he ducked under the couch.

Homer cawed. "Silly kitty."

Detective Sanchez let out a belly laugh. "With these two, who needs television!"

Miguel returned with a somber expression. "I hate to break up whatever party is happening here, but that was Delvecchio."

"Bad news?" Rosa asked.

Miguel nodded. "Enrique Vasquez has been shot dead in front of his house."

15

*R*osa frowned as she took in the bloodied figure of Enrique Vasquez lying face-down on the pavement beside his Sunliner in front of his house. She was on the scene with Miguel and Detective Sanchez, arriving moments before Dr. Philpott. Two police cruisers—American-style, painted black and white with large, rounded red lights on the roof—were there when they arrived. The scene was already roped off.

With his signature groan, Dr. Philpott lowered himself onto one knee to examine the body.

Rosa joined Miguel, who opened a palm. "We found this in his coat pocket."

Rosa wrinkled her nose at the small plastic bag filled with white powder. "Cocaine?"

"Appears to be. Maybe a few ounces. He could be dealing to individuals."

"I wonder if he was just leaving to meet up with someone," Rosa said. "Or if that person had come looking for goods and didn't get what they were hoping for."

One of the officers, dressed in a black uniform and police cap, approached Miguel. "We found the bullet, sir."

Miguel examined the offering. "Looks to be from a .45 revolver." He glanced at Rosa and Detective Sanchez. "Same as the last killing."

Detective Sanchez whistled. "Looky here." He reached under the foot pedals of the car and held out his finding. "Another creepy little doll."

"Perhaps more than one person is involved in these two killings," Rosa offered. "Is it Mob-related, as Bill suggested? Or some brujería cult?"

"Or both," Miguel said reluctantly.

"Looks pretty clear cut," Dr. Philpott said as he straightened up. "He most certainly died instantly. The bullet entered through the forehead and exited through the back." He pointed down at the blood-covered back of Enrique Vasquez's head. "He didn't know what hit him."

"A witness across the street heard a shot and

called it in," Miguel said. "Mrs. Paula MacDonald. She heard a car engine off in the distance heading north but didn't see it happen."

Officer Richardson had arrived with camera ready. Rosa gave him a friendly nod with a show of empty hands—a silent truce. Hoping to get on the man's good side, she stepped aside as he snapped photographs using his Busch Pressman camera with its top-of-the-line, front-facing accordion lens.

She wasn't being entirely altruistic—her own efforts photographing Salvador Vasquez's death had produced few results.

"Which house does Mrs. MacDonald live in?" Rosa asked.

Miguel pointed. "The one on the corner with the blue patio railing."

Rosa linked her arm in his. "Shall we?"

They strolled toward the MacDonald residence, breaking away as they reached the patio. Rosa stepped behind Miguel as he knocked on the door. It was opened by a housewife, who, by the look of flour dust in her graying-blond hair and the sweet aroma in the air, was in the middle of baking.

Miguel made introductions, then said, "We're sorry to interrupt, but if you could give us a moment of your time, it would be appreciated."

"Come in. I'm baking cookies for the grandkiddies. I babysit after school."

The house looked lived in, overfull with furniture and knickknacks. Rosa deduced that the MacDonalds were the type of people who threw nothing away. Following Mrs. MacDonald into a sunny kitchen, they took the proffered chairs.

"Like I already told those other police," Mrs. MacDonald said, "I thought a car had backfired. We get a lot of those on these streets now. Souped-up engines. Make a racket. I happened to be looking out the window and saw poor Mr. Vasquez fall to the ground. At first, I thought it was a heart attack. Mr. Kosse from next door had one last year, you know . . ." Mrs. MacDonald placed a plate of chocolate-chip cookies in front of them. "Please take one," she said, and without skipping a beat continued, ". . . but then I thought to myself, no, Mr. Vasquez is far too young for that."

"Did you see anyone else on the street?" Miguel asked, chewing his cookie.

"Well, I wasn't really looking." Mrs. MacDonald sat in one of the empty chairs. "But I saw a man through the sheers. Same ilk as Mr. Vasquez. He took off like a shot, and I thought, maybe I should go out there, see if Mr. Vasquez was reviving." She clicked her tongue, her eyes darkening as she remembered. "I got about six feet away from him and saw a big ol' hole in his head and blood everywhere. I'm not ashamed to say I screamed."

"I imagine it was very shocking," Rosa said. "Are you sure you're all right now?"

"Oh yes. It's not like I haven't seen blood before. I grew up on a farm, but it was just the initial shock of it. Well, I could see there'd be no reviving of Mr. Vasquez. I ran straight to the telephone and called the police."

"Do you think you could pick out the man you saw in a lineup?" Miguel asked.

Mrs. MacDonald shook her head. "He was across the street, and my long-distance eyesight isn't that good."

The timer on her stove went off, and she jumped to her feet. "Oh deary, my grandkiddies will be unhappy if I let these burn."

"Thanks for your help, Mrs. MacDonald," Miguel said. "We'll let ourselves out."

"Do you mind if I take a cookie for Detective Belmonte's partner?"

"Be my guest," Mrs. MacDonald said.

Rosa grabbed the cookie for Detective Sanchez

and was rewarded with a beaming grin when she offered it.

"Thanks, Miss Reed!" he said, wasting no time taking his first bite. "I was feeling the need for a little sustenance."

Rosa's gaze landed on the brown envelope Bill Sanchez carried—the enigmatic little dolls.

"Bill, can I have a look at the doll again?" Rosa asked.

Detective Sanchez handed her the envelope. Without touching it, Rosa committed the object to memory. It resembled the first doll, about five inches tall, made of rags and darning thread, except this one had been given cowboy boots.

Rosa handed the envelope back to Detective Sanchez. "I think I'm going to make a trip to the library."

Miguel's eyes twinkled as he stared back at her. "Our favorite place."

The Santa Bonita Library had played a big part in their early relationship in the forties. They had had their first conversation in the ancient history section when she was a teen and he a young soldier, sharing their first kiss in the garden at the back. Their love affair had been expressly forbidden by Rosa's domineering guardian, her Aunt Louisa Forrester. Even now, memories of that conflict caused Rosa's chest to tighten.

The end of the war had separated her and Miguel. She returned to her parents in London, and the distance proved too formidable. Life after heartache continued, and Rosa gave up on ever seeing Miguel again. A broken engagement had brought her back to Santa Bonita, and the rest, as they say, was history.

Rosa reached for her new husband's hand. "I'd love to meet you in the park again, but I'm going to do some research."

"Brujería?"

"It may be nothing, but I'm curious," she said.

Miguel gave her a quick kiss on the cheek. "I need to stay here until everything's cleaned up." He handed Rosa the keys to his Plymouth. "Sanchez can drive me home later."

$\mathcal{L}$ ooking more like an old wooden homestead home painted whiter than a government building, the Santa Bonita Library was one of the oldest buildings in town. Rosa tugged on the brass handle of the heavy door and was immediately hit with the heady smell of old books, a scent that made her feel warm and cozy inside. A staple in the library since Rosa had been a teen, the spinster librarian, Miss Cumberbatch, was as old as the hills. She glanced over the glasses perched on the tip of her nose, her eyes wrinkling as she smiled.

"Hello, Miss Cumberbatch," Rosa said quietly.

"Hello, Miss Reed," she said in a low whisper. "How was your trip to London?"

"Lovely," Rosa returned. "I spent a lot of time with my parents."

"Family is so important. Did you get to tour around the city? I imagine it's old hat to you. I've never been, though I've read books and seen photographs."

"I did visit some of the old haunts," Rosa said, omitting it was Miguel she'd been showing around.

"I've always wanted to go," Miss Cumberbatch said wistfully, "but at least I can travel through books." She peered over her glasses. "What wondrous topic are you desiring to research today?"

Rosa was unlike her contemporaries, who frequented the romance novel section or thumbed through the many copies of Dr. Spock on childcare. To Miss Cumberbatch's delight, the books Rosa had signed out in the past were *The Basics of Ballistics*, *Criminal Anthropology*, and *The Biography of H.H. Holmes*.

"You'll love this one, Miss Cumberbatch," Rosa said. "Brujería."

"Ooh," Miss Cumberbatch purred. "South American witchcraft. This way."

Rosa knew this library like the back of her hand and could easily find the cult and occult section, but she wouldn't have denied Miss Cumberbatch the obvious joy she found in leading the way and demonstrating her expertise.

The librarian ran her finger along the spines of several books before removing a hardcover entitled *Sorcery and Witchcraft in Ancient Mesoamerica.*

"This is a good place to start," she said, handing it to Rosa.

"Thank you, Miss Cumberbatch."

"Happy to help, Miss Reed. Anytime."

Rosa thumbed through the book, agreeing it was what she was looking for. She'd take the thick book back to her office where she could read with a cup of tea in her hand and a cat warming her lap.

Rosa signed out the book, almost making it to the door when she returned to the checkout desk. "Might I have a look at your telephone book, Miss Cumberbatch?"

The librarian opened a desk drawer, removed the directory, and handed it to Rosa. Rosa found the name Delgado. Next to the names of Alfonso and his wife, Fabiana, who was the secretary for MexAmera Trade Solutions, was their home address.

Diego would have to wait for his snuggles a little longer.

· · ·

As Rosa backed the Plymouth into a tight spot down the street from the Delgado residence in a lower-middle-class area, she saw a man exit the front door. Dressed in an embroidered, western-style silk shirt similar to the one Enrique Vasquez had worn, the man wore snakeskin cowboy boots. A long scar ran down his cheek.

It was the man she'd seen parked on the street the night of Salvador's murder—*it had to be*! Rosa put the car in park, grabbed her satchel, and ran as best she could in her heels toward the building. She just caught the man's retreating form as he rounded the far corner of the street and disappeared.

"Hey!" Rosa rounded the corner in time to watch him close the driver's door of a black Ford sedan about forty yards away. She fumbled for her camera but didn't quite get it out in time. The passenger window was open, and as he drove past, Rosa yelled, "Hey, mister!"

The man turned to her voice, his face crumpling into a scowl, but drove on without stopping.

Rosa memorized the license plate, then returned to the apartment building.

Inside, she found the appropriate apartment and knocked. An attractive woman in her late thirties, dressed in denim shorts and a cotton blouse unbuttoned halfway, the ends tied in a bow, opened the door. She regarded Rosa with a mild sense of concern.

"Mrs. Delgado?"

"Who's asking?"

"I'm Rosa Reed. I'm a private investigator working in conjunction with the Santa Bonita Police."

The woman narrowed her glassy brown eyes, the pupils so large they appeared almost black. "A woman gumshoe? Well, that's interesting. Hey." She snapped her fingers and pointed at Rosa. "You were at the birthday party at Maria Belmonte's."

"I was. I happened to notice you were there too. I understand that you work for MexAmera Trade Solutions. No one answered when I called earlier. I chanced dropping by. I hope this isn't a bad time."

"Sure. I'm, uh, just finishing my calisthenics. Come in."

The woman had a slim figure, and even with little makeup on, and messy hair, Rosa guessed that a middle-aged man, or even a younger man, might find Mrs. Delgado attractive. If the man with the scar had been here, Rosa doubted calisthenics had created the tousled look.

Rosa followed the woman into a small living room and took a proffered chair.

"Should I make coffee?" Mrs. Delgado asked.

"No, thank you, but kind of you to offer," Rosa said. "I won't be staying long." She reached into her purse and pulled out her notepad.

A package of cigarettes and a lighter lay on a small table at Mrs. Delgado's elbow. She picked them up, slipped out a cigarette, and lit it. Rosa's gaze landed on a film of white dust on the table's rim. Had Mrs. Delgado attempted to quickly brush the substance away before answering the door? If she and the man Rosa had seen leaving had been using cocaine, where had they gotten it from? Enrique Vasquez? How many dealers could there be in a small town like Santa Bonita?

"I don't think I know anything that will help you find Mr. Vasquez's killer," Mrs. Delgado said after blowing smoke at the yellowing ceiling. "Terrible news."

"How did you learn of Salvador Vasquez's death?"

She sniffed. "Mr. Rennings told me. About a minute before he fired me."

"I'm sorry to hear that," Rosa said. Though the way Mr. Rennings had made his feelings about the secretary known, she wasn't surprised.

"That's okay," Mrs. Delgado said with an exaggerated sigh. "I was tired of that job anyway. And Alfonso hated it when I worked. You know how men are. Thinks it looks poorly on him, like he doesn't make enough money to support a wife or something. Not that I'm seeing much of his cheddar now."

Rosa nodded. It was a common sentiment. "Do you remember what the time was when you left the party?"

"Margarita's birthday party? Nine or so."

"Did you come straight home?"

"Yes."

"How long did you work for MexAmera Trade Solutions?" Rosa asked, changing the subject.

"One stupid year."

"Why do you think Mr. Rennings fired you?"

"He told me he didn't think it was a good fit. Too bad, but it's his funeral. Oops, I guess that's not appropriate to say right now, is it?"

"Who was the man I saw leaving your house?"

For a moment, the woman just stared at Rosa with her eyes narrowed and her mouth half open in an expression of surprise, anger, and perhaps a little fear.

"I don't know what this has to do with anything. Am I a suspect? I'd rather talk to a *real* police officer.

And what happens in my home isn't any of *your* business."

Rosa reminded her, "I've been asked to consult on this case. I'm here because someone killed Salvador Vasquez, and I, along with the police, am looking for the killer. You were overheard having a bitter argument with him, and he knew something that you didn't want anyone to know about." Rosa looked at her steadily. "I gather your husband doesn't know about your *friend*."

Mrs. Delgado tapped her cigarette over the glass ashtray on the table. "My husband only cares about one thing, Miss Reed, betting on the horses. He wouldn't notice me meeting with anyone unless it had four legs and a mane."

"Does your husband know the man who was here?"

"No. I met Alex at an LA party a month ago."

"A party?"

"Yeah, it's just . . ." Mrs. Delgado waved her hand dismissively. "An old school friend had a birthday. Anyway, Alex isn't from around here. He's never met my husband or anyone else I know from Santa Bonita."

"Was that Alex I saw leaving your building as I drove up?"

Mrs. Delgado's mouth formed a hard line as a blush crept up her neck. She looked as if she was about to "flip her lid," as Clarence liked to say. Instead, she broke eye contact and stared out the window.

"I have no idea who you saw."

"Does he drive a black Ford sedan?"

"I think he drives a white Chevrolet or something." She looked defiantly at Rosa. But Rosa could tell she was disturbed by that question.

"Was he parked out on the street the night of the birthday party?"

"What? No. I don't know. If he was, he didn't tell me."

"Is he the one providing you with . . ." Rosa nodded to the white powder residue on the table.

"What? That? No!" Mrs. Delgado used a tissue to abruptly brush the white powder to the floor. "That's rat poison. I told you, Alfonso didn't care that I live in a dump now."

Rosa would hardly consider the modest house a dump, nor did she fall for Mrs. Delgado's obvious fib. "I'll be needing Alex's last name and his contact information."

Mrs. Delgado took a final puff on her cigarette

before aggressively stubbing it out in the ashtray. "His name is Deleon. I don't know where he lives."

"Do you or your husband own a gun?"

"*What?* No!" she said incredulously. "I know what you're getting at, and you're way off the mark. I certainly did not shoot my boss, and neither did Alfonso! I've never shot a gun in my life, and I don't think my husband has either." She scoffed. "He'd be too scared to."

"Do you know much about Mexican witchcraft?"

Mrs. Delgado let out a dry chuckle. "You're all over the map, aren't you?"

"Talismans, things of that nature?" Rosa pressed. She watched for a telltale reaction, but if the mention of those things struck home, Mrs. Delgado hid it well.

"I never even knew there were such things." She shifted to the edge of her seat, a sure signal she was eager for this interview to end.

"One last question for now," Rosa said. "Did you know Enrique Vasquez?"

"Who? Oh, wait. Mr. Vasquez had a brother or cousin by that name."

"A brother. He was murdered yesterday."

Mrs. Delgado narrowed her eyes again, and she cocked her head. "Such bad luck, huh?"

Rosa looked pointedly at the remnants of the white dust on the side table. "He's been known to sell drugs."

Mrs. Delgado swallowed. "I wouldn't know anything about that. Besides, I was with Alex all day yesterday. But, if you're looking for someone with a motive, why don't you talk to Simon Rennings?"

"I already have."

"I'll bet he didn't tell you about his wife and Salvador."

"Why?" Rosa asked. "Were they involved too?" How many affairs could the small staff in one office have?

"Not really. But Mrs. Rennings had feelings for Mr. Vasquez. She told me so herself. It drove Mr. Rennings mad with jealousy. Mr. Vasquez was a very smooth, handsome man. You must've met him, right? Far too old for me, mind you, but I can see why women were attracted to him. Every time Mrs. Rennings came to the office, she openly flirted with him. Once, after she left and Mr. Vasquez went out to see a client, I saw Mr. Rennings fly into a rage. He didn't know that I had heard him. I hadn't left for lunch yet." Like a cat who caught the mouse, she leaned in. "I heard him say out loud that he was going to kill Mr. Vasquez someday."

The story seemed too convenient. However, many a murder had been committed at the hand of a jealous spouse.

Even so, this motive didn't appear to be connected with Enrique's murder, but it was worth noting for later consideration.

Mrs. Delgado wasn't finished. "Mr. Rennings was always quite proud of his gun collection," she said. "He goes to the gun range to blow off steam."

If this was true, then Mr. Rennings had out and out lied about not owning a gun. But why?

The telephone rang, and Rosa got to her feet. "I'll see myself out."

Mrs. Delgado nodded in gratitude, then disappeared into the kitchen.

A wall hanging was pinned to the wall behind the door. The brightly colored, Spanish-looking piece of woven art depicted a woman rising from the ground. Her torso and face were human, but she had gray-and-black ornately decorated moth wings instead of arms. Her legs were those of an insect.

The phrase *la cambiaformas* was woven in bright-red thread underneath the odd-looking moth woman. Shape-shifter?

Rosa glanced down the hall toward the kitchen, then took out her camera to snap a picture.

as Rosa drove away, the sight of a cat zipping across the street made her think of Diego and she returned to Miguel's house to check on him. Miguel had given her a key, and Rosa felt a buzz of excitement as she let herself into his house. *Her* house. And soon, after this blasted second wedding, she'd make a public claim to it, instead of feeling like she had as a teen, sneaking around with Miguel.

Homer was in his cage looking well behaved, but Diego was nowhere to be found.

"Diego?" Rosa put the library book on the coffee table as she scoured the living room. "Diego," she sang, "Where are you?"

After a tour throughout the house and still no

Diego, Rosa felt the pinching of alarm. Had her pet gotten out? He'd be all right if he had, wouldn't he?

"Diego!"

Homer repeated, "Diego."

With one hand on her hip, she said, "Have you seen him, Homer? Where is Diego?"

"Silly cat," he cawed. "Silly cat."

Then, as if Rosa hadn't been frantically looking, Diego sauntered out from wherever he'd been hiding with all his feline sophistication, stopped in the middle of the room, and stared.

"Where were you?" Rosa said. She swooped him up and nuzzled his furry body to her neck. "Don't scare me like that."

Now that she had been reassured of Diego's safety, Rosa made herself a cup of tea and settled into one of the living room chairs to read her library book on brujería. The ancient South American spiritualism was complex, and she found the information about the various cults and witchcraft fascinating. In light of this reference, Rosa wondered who the killer could be. Taking out her notebook and pen, she scribbled out the potential suspects. Diego immediately made a bed out of the library book she'd set aside.

Francisca Vasquez. The new wife of the first

victim. Perhaps she'd found out something distasteful about Salvador. Her husband mightn't have been as innocent as she liked to claim and more like his brother than she thought. Not a great motive, but the spouse can never be overlooked.

Simon Rennings. The under-appreciated employee whose wife had taken a shine to his boss. With apparent problems controlling his anger, the fact that he'd lied about gun ownership was troubling.

Fabiana Delgado. The bitter married secretary with a penchant for other men. For someone who feared a ruined reputation, she wasn't very careful about her assignations. Not only that, she also quite possibly had an addiction to drugs. Had Enrique cut her off? Mrs. Delgado had two separate yet plausible motives to kill both brothers.

Alex Deleon. The male friend of Fabiana Delgado, who shares a craving for cocaine? They'd have to keep an eye on him.

Miranda Vasquez Torres. Daughter of the first victim, niece of the second. Was she the one who argued with Salvador Vasquez on the night of the fiesta? And if so, what were they arguing about?

Rosa flipped back through the pages of her notebook to the one where she'd recorded her last conversation with Enrique Vasquez and noted the address he'd mentioned.

She lifted Diego off the library book, putting the volume into her handbag. "Do you want to go for a car ride?"

Rosa had half expected Miranda Vasquez Torres' address to be in some rundown part of Santa Bonita. She was surprised to find a reasonable-looking apartment building in the northwest end of town, perched on a craggy cliff with a view of a small beach and the Pacific Ocean below. Someone was looking after her. Her father?

Diego's head poked out of the satchel with curiosity. He shifted in the satchel, his weight pulling on Rosa's shoulders, and she set the satchel on the ground for a reprieve. A knock on the door brought no response, and Rosa was about to call it a day when she noticed a young woman sitting on a bench in a small park across the street. She was feeding breadcrumbs out of a brown paper bag to a squirrel who seemed happy to accept the easy lunch.

Rosa walked over to the park and approached the woman. Diego's green-gold eyes were round with interest in the furry creature, and Rosa had to tighten her hold on him.

"Hello, I'm looking for Miranda Vasquez Torres," she said.

Startled, the woman stared up at Rosa. "And you are?"

Rosa sat down beside her on the wooden bench. "My name is Rosa Reed, and this is Diego."

"I'm Miranda Vasquez Torres." With softening eyes, Miss Torres reached over to scratch Diego's head. "Hey there. You're a sweetie, aren't you?"

"He'd like you to believe it," Rosa said with a smile.

"So, Miss Reed," Miss Torres said, "why are you looking for me?"

Rosa said gently, "I'm a private investigator. On occasion, I consult with the police."

"And this is one of those occasions?"

"Yes."

Miss Torres looked up with round, questioning eyes. "Hey, how did you find me?"

"I spoke to your uncle Enrique."

"Ah, but why were you talking to him? He hasn't been arrested again, has he?"

"You haven't heard?"

"Heard what?"

Rosa hated this part of her job. She let out a breath, then began, "I'm afraid your father was murdered two nights ago in El Pequeño Barrio after attending a fiesta."

Miss Torres froze. "My dad's dead? How?"

"He was shot."

"I don't understand. Why would someone kill him?"

Rosa could only shrug.

Miss Torres tightly clasped her hands in her lap, her chin down and eyes pinched closed. Unsuccessfully, she tried to hold back tears.

"You were there, on the street, outside the house where the party took place," Rosa said, taking a chance. She hadn't seen the woman's face, but Miss Torres' voice sounded right. "I saw you arguing with your father."

"Yes, we were arguing. We always argued!"

At that moment, Miss Torres looked like a sad little street girl, lost and alone. How was Rosa going to tell her that her uncle had been murdered too?

Diego wiggled out of Rosa's satchel. As if he knew who needed him most, the cat pawed Miss Torres' lap, then climbed on. Miss Torres let out a sob and cried into his fur.

"He's a very nice cat," she said after a while. After

accepting a tissue from Rosa, she asked, "Who killed him?"

"We don't know yet. Did you see anything that night? Anybody?"

"No, I . . . just ran over to my bicycle and rode off. I was mad; we were arguing about money." She paused for a moment and wiped her eyes, "I'm having a hard life, Miss Reed. I need . . . things. My dad was giving me money, but I . . . I needed more."

Rosa had to consider the possibility this girl had killed her father for money to buy drugs. It wasn't beyond possibility; drugs were known to turn the most passive person into someone unrecognizably violent.

"How did you know your father would be at the fiesta that night?" she asked.

Miss Torres glanced away, shamefaced. "I followed him." Nuzzling Diego as if he was the giver of strength, Miss Torres continued, "I've been a terrible daughter. When Mom died when I was thirteen, I turned to drugs and alcohol to get by. It's wrong, but I'm so weak."

"There are places you can go for help," Rosa said. "I can get you a number to call. I can even take you there. I know the twelve-step program has had great results."

Miss Torres glanced sideways at Rosa. "You're a very kind lady, Miss Reed."

Rosa sat beside Miranda Vasquez Torres on the bench, looking over a small park. Gently, she guided the conversation back to the case. "Miss Torres, knowing what kind of people your uncle Enrique had worked with, do you think any of them had anything against your dad?"

"No, no one. Dad had nothing to do with Enrique or any of the thugs he hangs out with. My uncle has chosen an unfortunate way to make a living, but deep inside, he's a good guy."

She worked the tissue in her hands. Rosa noticed broken fingernails painted red. She was close to Rosa's age, but her face looked drawn and older.

"Did your uncle ever mention anybody that might be after *him*?"

"Not to me. He doesn't talk much about what he does."

Diego had curled up in a ball on Miss Torres' lap, his rhythmic breathing bringing a steady comfort. Rosa reached over with grateful affection and stroked his back.

"Miss Torres," she started. "Did anyone see you leave on your bike?"

"I don't know. I didn't notice anyone."

"Is your memory of that night clear? I'm sorry to have to ask this, but were you under the influence of drugs or alcohol?"

"I wasn't. Like I said, I ran out of money. I've been sober for a few days now." She held out a shaking palm. "See this? And I'm a mess. I don't sleep well, and when I do, I have horrific dreams."

"Sober? Good for you," Rosa said. "Do you happen to own a gun?"

"No."

Reluctant to utter the next words and dismayed that she had to be the one to deliver them, Rosa paused. "Miss Torres, I'm afraid I have more bad news. Do you think you'll be able to bear it?"

Miss Torres pulled Diego to her chest. "I'm not sure, Miss Reed, but whatever it is, I'd rather hear it from you."

"I'm sorry to have to tell you, but this morning, your uncle was also shot and killed."

Miranda silently wept into Diego's neck.

"I don't think you should be alone tonight, Miss Torres," Rosa said, providing more tissue.

Miranda Vasquez Torres stared back with red, bloodshot eyes. "I don't know anyone who can help me."

"I do." Rosa took the girl's hand. "The kind sisters at St. Francis Church."

18

The next morning, Rosa headed five miles south of town to the Santa Bonita Gun Club. It was not the first time Rosa had been to a gun range. Her parents had taught her to shoot when they'd spent summer holidays in the country, and she'd gained a reputation as a crack shot. She often carried her snub-nosed Smith and Wesson Colt Cobra .38 special in her bag.

She *was*, after all, the daughter of Ginger Gold.

The gun club included a one-story red-brick building that had once served as a military training facility. Rosa introduced herself at the reception area as a former police constable of London Metropolitan Police interested in keeping up her skills.

The middle-aged man at the reception desk, who looked much like a military man—fit, trim, and with short-cropped hair—seemed impressed with her credentials. He introduced himself as Retired Master Sergeant Hal Cummings and told her that the facility had indeed once served as a military facility for arms training.

"Would a Mr. Simon Rennings happen to be here?" Rosa asked. "He's a new acquaintance of mine."

"He is. He's a regular. I'll take you out to him."

Master Sergeant Cummings led her to the rear of the building and outside to a large field where a half dozen side-by-side brick construction booths faced targets of varying distances. Hanging from a system of cables and pulleys, the targets could be moved forward and back. Two shooters were practicing. One of them was Simon Rennings.

Master Sergeant Cummings went over the club guidelines for Rosa's benefit, gave her a set of earmuffs, and a choice between a Colt 'detective special' and a Smith and Wesson model 36.

Rosa chose the Colt then took the booth right beside Mr. Rennings, who was busy reloading his gun and didn't take notice. She adopted the proper shooter's stance: feet shoulder-width apart, one foot in front of the other, and knees slightly bent. She kept her shooting arm, her right, straight out in front of her at eye level, while the support arm was also slightly bent.

Under the watchful eye of Master Sergeant Cummings, Rosa aimed for the brightly colored paper target that hung about four yards away, scoring six rounds almost direct center.

"Miss Reed!" Master Sergeant Cummings flashed her a respectful grin. "If you're out of practice, I want to see you in action after you've warmed up! That is mighty fine shooting. Not many ladies come this way. In fact, there's only been one, an older gal, in the last week."

Rosa pushed a button on the wall, and the target went out three yards further. She reloaded from a box of bullets the master sergeant had given her, then shot six more direct hits.

This time Simon Rennings noticed.

As effusive and excited as a schoolboy who'd just won a football match, Master Sergeant Cummings turned to Rosa's neighbor. "Did you see that, Mr. Rennings?"

Mr. Rennings, having taken off his earmuffs, stared at Rosa with a look of dismay.

Rosa smiled brightly. "Hello, Mr. Rennings. Do you have a moment to chat?"

"I'll bid you both good day," the master sergeant said. "You know where to find me if you need me."

Mr. Rennings sneered at Rosa, laid his weapon down, and folded his arms. "I suppose you think you caught me in a lie."

Rosa laid her gun down as well. "Haven't I?"

After a shrug, he said, "So what? I wasn't under oath. We all have our secrets, don't we, *Miss* Reed?"

"Santa Bonita is a small town, indeed," Rosa returned with a frown. Had he somehow heard of her London wedding? If so, he wouldn't be the only one. Four weeks to the Catholic ceremony couldn't come fast enough. She pivoted the focus back to him. "It's come to my attention that Mrs. Rennings was infatuated with Salvador Vasquez and that you had quite a temper about it."

"You've been talking to that witch Delgado!"

"It doesn't matter who I've been talking to if it's true. The police will discover the facts one way or another."

"Look here, I lied about guns and knowing how to shoot because I was afraid of how it would look . . . with Mr. Vasquez shot dead and me being the last to see him and all."

Rosa wondered how the man thought he'd keep this information from the police as he clearly had made a name for himself at the firing range. Scared people do irrational things. So do guilty ones.

"If I were you, I'd be prepared to make an account of all the firearms you own, Mr. Rennings."

"I told you, I didn't kill him. You can take that to the bank."

"A witness claims to have heard you threaten him."

Mr. Rennings grunted. "You can't believe anything that adulteress has to say. She's a liar, a proven liar!"

"So are you."

Mr. Rennings rapped his knuckles on the counter, then strode angrily away. Rosa exhaled then headed back to her car. If she didn't hurry, she'd be late to a planned lunch she and Miguel had with Mrs. Belmonte, and that wouldn't do.

"It's so nice that you could come!" Mrs. Belmonte said as she put yet another plate full of delicious breakfast burritos on the dining room table in front of Rosa. Already on the table was a pitcher of freshly squeezed orange juice, a pot of coffee, and a bowl of fresh fruit, including cut watermelon and oranges.

Rosa wondered who on earth would eat all that food, but then she noticed Miguel was about to start on his second burrito.

"I like this idea of mixing breakfast with lunch," Mrs. Belmonte said as she poured Miguel a cup of coffee. "I never heard of 'brunch' before I came to the USA. I have some rice leftovers. Should I bring it too?"

Rosa waved her hands. "Oh, no thank you. Not for me."

"I'm not sure about this brunch idea," Miguel said as he swallowed a mouthful. "You have to survive until ten thirty, and you don't eat again until supper. I'm like a machine. I need fuel to run."

"A machine?" Mrs. Belmonte raised her eyebrows. "You and your brothers were more like animals at the table."

"Mamá, come on!" Miguel spread his hands and nodded to Rosa. "She doesn't need to hear that. Are you trying to scare her off?"

"She needs to know the truth! She can take it." Mrs. Belmonte turned to Rosa. "All of my sons can put away my burritos like they are afraid of a cold winter coming."

"Maybe Hector, he's always been a little fat," Miguel observed.

"Miguel!" Mrs. Belmonte exclaimed.

"But look at me," Miguel continued undeterred, as he leaned back and patted his belly. "I am *el guapo*. The most handsome man in the family!"

Rosa giggled.

"Si, you are handsome like your father," Mrs. Belmonte conceded as she sliced an apple, "but Mario is funnier."

"He is not!" Miguel said, obviously offended.

"Besides, look at that nice Detective Sanchez that Carlotta is dating," Mrs. Belmonte continued, after blowing on her coffee. "He is not *extremely* handsome—nice looking, polite, *and* a very successful police detective!"

Miguel looked baffled, "How do you know how successful he is?"

"Because he told me. *And* he dresses nicely too! You could take some lessons."

Rosa and Miguel shared an incredulous look. All the credit for Detective Sanchez's improved wardrobe went to Carlotta.

"Yes, he smokes a bit too much." As if sharing a confidential secret, Mrs. Belmonte lowered her voice and leaned closer to Rosa. "But Carlotta will love him so much, he will eventually stop doing that. Love always wins." She nodded confidently. "I think they'll have adorable babies." She clapped her hands. "Now, we must talk about your wedding. Father Navarro will arrange everything, yes?"

Rosa glanced at Miguel but stayed quiet. This was one topic she would let him take the lead on.

"Father Navarro needs to consult with the bishop," Miguel said.

Mrs. Belmonte's expression dropped. "It's not going to be a problem, is it? You must marry in the Church!"

"Mamá, it won't be a problem. Father Navarro reassured us that he can make sure the wedding happens on the date we chose. First week in April, right?"

Mrs. Belmonte relaxed. "*Muy bien*. We will be a happy family on that day. Rosa, you must pick bridesmaids and colors for your dresses."

"I will have two bridesmaids," Rosa said. "My cousin Gloria and Carlotta."

Mrs. Belmonte beamed. "It will be a good rehearsal for Carlotta, soon to be a bride, I hope. And colors?"

"I'm not sure yet," Rosa said. "I want to talk it

over with my mother. She owns a dress shop, so she'll have good ideas."

"I will meet your mother and father, yes? They are coming to the wedding?"

Rosa had the sensation of one being trapped. "Well, it's a long journey from London."

Mrs. Belmonte protested. "But the airplanes, they make it go fast."

"Yes, but my father's doctor has recommended he not fly. But it's all right, Mrs. Belmonte. We'll hire a photographer and send photos."

"It's not the same as being here. You're sure—"

"Mamá," Miguel interrupted. "Mr. and Mrs. Reed can't come, so we must make the best of it."

"Of course," Mrs. Belmonte said with a sigh. "But the church will look lopsided with so much family on your side and hardly any on Rosa's."

"The most important thing is that the ceremony happens," Miguel said.

"After the wedding, I want you to come and have brunch at the Forresters'," Rosa said, hoping to change the subject. "You can sample Señora Gomez's huevos rancheros."

"Si, si, I would like that, but . . . who is Señora Gomez?" Mrs. Belmonte's smile was brilliant.

"She's the head housekeeper and cook," Rosa said.

Mrs. Belmonte's chin dropped, and she shot a look at Miguel. "You will have servants?"

Miguel's eyes flashed with the same trapped look Rosa had felt.

"Well, *we* won't," he said.

"At least not to begin with," Rosa added.

Miguel glanced at her sideways. A warning look?

Rosa ignored it and continued. "I had a nanny growing up, Nanny Green, and she was wonderful. She was a great companion and taught me a lot."

Mrs. Belmonte narrowed her eyes, looking unimpressed. "Mexican women raise their own children."

"Oh, I was raised by my mother and father," Rosa said. "They both worked, so it was nice to have Nanny when they weren't around."

Rosa's words failed to mollify her mother-in-law.

Mrs. Belmonte appealed to her son. "Your wife isn't going to *work*, is she? A wife is meant to care for the home. Who's going to cook for you?"

Rosa was aware of the social expectations for women, and not a lot had changed since her mother was a young woman. Such conventions had never stopped Ginger, and Rosa wouldn't let them stop her either.

"We don't know what we'll end up doing yet,"

Rosa said lightly, forcing a smile. "I do know one thing, though. If I'm to be the one cooking, Miguel won't have any worries about becoming plump like Hector."

Miguel laughed stiffly, squeezing Rosa's hand. Mrs. Belmonte seemed to get the message and pressed her lips together. "So, Mamá, have you heard from Carlotta?" he said, changing the subject. "She and Detective Sanchez seem happy."

At least Mrs. Belmonte had the grace to change the subject. "Detective Sanchez is a nice man and good for Carlotta. I hope to hear happy news from them too. But not too soon now. One wedding at a time."

"That would be lovely," Rosa offered.

Mrs. Belmonte nodded, her eyes not entirely free of the suspicion of Rosa's future intentions. She reached for Miguel's hand. "You have a good job, Miguel. It's so nice of your chief to let you have some time to visit your mother. Have you found the wicked person who killed poor Salvador yet?"

"Well . . ." Miguel sighed, "it's a confusing one all right. You know I can't discuss the case in detail with you, Mamá, but basically, we have two brothers murdered by gunshot within a day and a half of each other. So far, no witnesses, even though there were lots of people around.

"*Infamante.*" Mrs. Belmonte shook her head, "Shameful."

"And there might be some kind of brujería connection," Miguel said.

"Brujería?" Mrs. Belmonte crossed herself.

"I'm just starting to research now," Rosa said. "I took a book out of the library."

"This is evil. I don't like this." Mrs. Belmonte shook her head and scowled. "How could Salvador be a part of something like that?"

"At this point, we don't know if he was," Rosa answered. "We're guessing the person who killed him was."

"I remember when we were in Mexico, there was an old lady in our village who everyone said was *una bruja,* a witch. She made strange little dolls and put them in her window."

Rosa and Miguel looked at each other.

"Dolls?" Miguel asked.

"Well, kind of like a doll, but not really. I don't know the English word. But they were made just out of different colored cloth. She used thread for the eyes and the hair. It was spooky; sometimes, the dolls looked like people in the village. It was creepy.

One time, she made a doll that looked like *el alcalde*, the town mayor. She put the doll in her window, and he died one day later. We all saw it. That same doll was found on the floor next to the mayor. But of course, the police could not charge the woman since he died of a heart attack." Mrs. Belmonte shook her head again. "He was a nice man. Everyone thought so. Terrible shame." She shivered. "I remember now, a disturbing drawing on the door. Half woman, half moth."

Rosa glanced at Miguel, then reached into her bag and took out the photo she had snapped and later developed in her office darkroom.

"Like this?"

Mrs. Belmonte gasped and crossed herself again. "*¡Ay, Dios mío!*"

Rosa grabbed Miguel's hand. "We have to talk."

19

"You can stay here to talk about your very important police matters," Mrs. Belmonte said, looking very much like she could use some air. "I have to deliver these leftover burritos to Consuela Gonzales. The poor woman doesn't cook much anymore, and she's getting too thin." Miguel's mother gathered up the plates and disappeared into the kitchen.

"I didn't mean to frighten your mother with the picture," Rosa said.

"I'm a little surprised by her reaction. My mom has strong convictions when it comes to faith, but I wouldn't call her superstitious." He motioned to the photograph. "Where did you take that?"

"At Fabiana Delgado's house," Rosa said. "In the hallway by the front door."

Miguel blew air out of his cheeks. *"Por todos los santos*, this case is confusing. What could Fabiana Delgado possibly have to do with Enrique Vasquez? As far as we know, they didn't even know each other."

Rosa rested a palm on Miguel's shoulder. "Have you completed all the interviews connected with the Enrique Vasquez murder?"

"Almost. Sanchez is finishing that up today. So far, he's had nothing to report. Without even one witness, there is not much to go on."

"How about the casing from the bullet?"

"Like Salvador Vasquez, this casing came from a Colt .38. Colts have a left barrel twist instead of right like most other makes. Reminds me of you Brits driving on the wrong side of the road."

Rosa was aware of this fact but laughed at Miguel's analogy. "You're almost as funny as Mario."

"He doesn't have the same delivery as I do."

"You *are* the most handsome Belmonte brother, though." She kissed him on the cheek. "Your mamá is right about that."

"Flattery will get you everywhere, Mrs. Belmonte."

"Shh!" Rosa glanced toward the kitchen, relieved to find it quiet. "Don't let your mother hear you call me that."

Miguel moved in closer. "We're alone."

"Not for long. *Mrs. Belmonte* will be back soon." Rosa playfully nudged Miguel away. "Back to the case. It's unfortunate that Colt revolvers are very common in this state."

"True," Miguel said. "Philpott hasn't released the report on Salvador's cause of death yet, either."

Rosa furrowed her brow. "That's odd. He's usually done in a day or two. Are there other murder cases ahead in line or a multiple death event I haven't heard about?"

"No, there isn't," Miguel said with a shake of his head. "He told me he needs to check on something before filing an official cause of death report. When I pressed, he said he'd rather wait until he had something conclusive."

"But a bullet through the head . . ."

"Yeah, you'd think that it's pretty clear-cut. He said as much at the scene. He's also working on Enrique's postmortem."

"I had an interesting encounter with Mr. Rennings this morning." Rosa filled Miguel in on the details of the exchange at the gun range.

Miguel frowned. "You were alone on a gun range with a possible killer who was in possession of a gun?"

"*I* was also in possession of a gun," Rosa said. "And we weren't alone. Other people were practicing, and the master sergeant was there."

"I'll send some guys over to check Rennings's gun collection. If we find a Colt, then we'll need to dig a bit deeper. As for Fabiana Delgado, maybe I should have her movements monitored. If she's involved in a Mexican death cult or some other strange thing, there's a good chance she'll lead us to the others."

Rosa reached into her bag and pulled out *Sorcery and Witchcraft in Ancient Mesoamerica* and turned to the section on iconography. "I borrowed this from the library."

She flipped the pages until she pointed to a full-page picture of the same half woman, half moth creature that hung on Mrs. Delgado's wall.

"That's pretty creepy-looking, all right," Miguel remarked as he leaned in to look.

"There's more." Rosa continued to flip the pages until she came to a section called "The Shape-Shifters." She tapped her finger on the page. "Centuries ago, a very distinct cult arose among the Mayans and some of the Aztecs. This was long before the Conquistadors came. Long before there was ever such thing as a Mexican!"

Miguel pointed to the headline and whistled. "La cambiaformas."

"That's what it says on Mrs. Delgado's wall hanging."

"The witches who practiced this cult believed that with the proper incantations, they could change into a moth," Rosa said, reading aloud. "And then quickly transform back into a woman again. Some branches of the cult worshipped jaguars and other animals, but the main branch stuck with moths. Moth worshippers never look in a mirror. That was the case even before glass mirrors were invented, when mirrors were polished metal. They believed that the spirits that they called upon to help them would steal their souls if they did. According to them, a mirror doesn't show a reflection, but rather an impostor, an evil spirit who could claim the right to their soul."

Miguel grinned lopsidedly. "So, you could recognize them by their poor grooming?"

Rosa laughed. "They did their best by using polished volcanic obsidian. The belief was that a spirit couldn't reach out from anything that had been so recently in the fires of hell."

Miguel's forehead buckled. "Okay."

Rosa continued. "They also believed that using talismans could aid them in harming or even killing individuals. Some of them used cloth to make talismans of their intended victims and would leave the doll-like image on murdered victims' bodies or hide it somewhere among their personal possessions. They believed the talisman would act as a kind of facilitator for the murder."

"Warming the atmosphere up before the big event?"

"Something like that," Rosa said. "But the strange thing is, the murder could only happen on certain days of the month or even in certain years, or when the intended victim reached a certain age."

"And who decided that?" Miguel asked.

"It was determined by occult methods like rolling bones or laying the cards."

"Oh man," Miguel said, leaning back on the couch. "What are we into here?"

"If we are to follow this line of investigation, we'd have to eliminate all our male suspects," Rosa said. "The witches were always women. If you wanted someone to die back in Mesoamerica in fifteen hundred BC, you could pay a witch to kill for you."

Miguel thought for a moment. "So, if we follow

this line of investigation, a woman who is part of this ancient cambiaformas cult could've been hired by drug smugglers or others with nefarious intent to kill Enrique but first killed Salvador by mistake?"

"Perhaps, perhaps not," Rosa said. "The hire could've been for both brothers. It depends on the motive."

Miguel snapped his fingers. "Maybe Simon Rennings hired Fabiana Delgado to do the job!"

"Yes, that is a possibility," Rosa admitted. "He has a motive to kill Salvador, but what did he have against Enrique?"

20

*A*fter leaving a note for Mrs. Belmonte, Rosa and Miguel returned to the scene of the latest murder. Enrique Vasquez had lived in the kind of neighborhood embodied in the "American Dream." Everywhere Rosa looked, there were small but well-kept lawns in front of medium-sized, one-story houses. Miguel confirmed people who lived there earned decent wages and were predominantly Caucasian. With his darker skin and accented speech, Enrique Vasquez would've stood out in this area of town.

School was in session, so no kids were to be seen, but Rosa noted several hopscotch grids drawn in white chalk along the palm-tree-lined street. There was nothing new to note besides the bloodstain that hadn't got thoroughly washed off the pavement.

"Sanchez said all the neighbors were interviewed," Miguel said. "No one saw anything."

"It doesn't hurt to try again," Rosa said.

Miguel scratched his temple. "Memories are often refreshed after a bit of time passes."

Rosa had found that to be true. There was nothing like a frightful murder with an unknown killer to seal the lips.

Before they could choose a door to knock on, a fellow from across the street stepped out onto his porch, Bing Crosby singing the tune "Chattanooga Shoeshine Boy," following him outside. In his midfifties, the man wore dark slacks, a button-down shirt, and leaned on a cane. His close-cropped, graying hair was in the same military style as the manager of the gun club Rosa had visited that morning. With his free hand, he cupped a palm over his eyes to shield the sun. "Howdy?" He regarded Rosa with friendly eyes, but when he took in Miguel, they shadowed with suspicion. "You lost?"

"Good afternoon, sir," Miguel started. "I'm Detective Belmonte with the Santa Bonita Police, and this is . . ."

He glanced at Rosa, and she held in a smirk. Her

new husband had yet to formally introduce her in a work-related situation.

She came to his rescue. "I'm Rosa Reed, a private investigator consulting with the police."

The man grunted before responding. "Allen Fisher, retired major, US Army. Can't imagine why you're snooping about. I know I haven't done anything illegal, and I'll bet Bob Wilson next door hasn't nor Fred Tarkenton two houses down from me, so I'm going to assume this is about the Vasquez fellow across the road. Am I right?"

"Yes, it is," Miguel said with a challenging look. "But why would you say that?"

Rosa's heart skipped a beat. The last thing she wanted was a showdown over race.

"No reason," Mr. Fisher said. "Just gotta wonder how a fella like that could afford a house in this neighborhood, huh? Bad money, *that's* how."

"How well did you know Mr. Vasquez?" Miguel asked.

The man readjusted his weight on his cane. "Look, I know what happened to Enrique Vasquez. But I didn't see anything. I wasn't even home." He pointed to his weak leg. "At the doc's place."

"Did you know that Mr. Vasquez's brother was also shot down?" Rosa said.

He shook his head. "Sorry to hear that, miss."

"You've got a good view of Enrique Vasquez's house," Miguel said. "Are you sure you didn't see anything unusual or suspicious in the last few days?"

"With *those* people, there's always something unusual or suspicious, Detective."

Rosa admired how Miguel took the slight on the chin. The criminal element ran through all races.

Calmly, Miguel asked, "Can you be more specific, Mr. Fisher?"

"Well, he'd get company, fellows in flashy clothes. They would show up here, sometimes five of them at once and disappear into his house. They'd turn on that Mexican music, loud. Not sure how they could think, much less talk. If they were trying to be inconspicuous, they did a poor job of it."

"Did you ever speak to any of them?" Rosa asked.

"Heck, no."

"Did you ever see anyone carry a gun?"

"Actually, yes. Just as two of them were entering the house one day, I was sitting here on the front patio. They didn't look this way, so they didn't see me. One guy took off his jacket, and I saw a Colt revolver tucked into his waistband."

"Would you be able to identify any of them if you were shown a picture?"

"I might. The war took my leg, but my eyesight is just fine."

Rosa described Alex Deleon, who she'd seen now on two suspicious occasions.

"Well, they all look alike to me, but there's no missing that scar. He's the fellow with the Colt revolver."

21

The Santa Bonita Police Department was housed in a single-level Spanish mission-style building with arches and a red-clay tile roof. The word "quaint" came to Rosa's mind, especially when she recalled its formal counterparts found in London.

There was an open area filled with desks occupied by uniform-wearing officers, but Miguel had his own office down the hall, partitioned from the rest by frosted glass and a wood-veneer door. Inside were functional items like a desk, filing cabinets, and a blackboard.

Miguel closed the blinds against the sun, then picked up a piece of chalk. He wrote the name *Alex*

Deleon in big block letters. Under that, he scribbled "Colt."

"We have a witness who claims to have seen him at the second murder victim's house with a Colt on his person, the same type of gun used to bring down both brothers. What else?"

"I saw him leave Fabiana Delgado's house," Rosa said, taking a seat in one of the chairs facing Miguel's desk. "She was rather disheveled, so unless he'd wrestled her down for something, his being there was probably for a romantic rendezvous rather than a business meeting. Mrs. Delgado has motive for killing Salvador Vasquez."

Miguel drew arrows on the blackboard connecting Mrs. Delgado to Salvador Vasquez. "Romantically involved with the secretary of victim one, who has motive. But why would she kill Enrique Vasquez too?"

"Her motive could be cult-related," Rosa said, "and if that's the case, her reasons may not make rational sense.

Miguel brushed chalk dust off his hands. "She could be a brujería assassin of some kind, and the wall hanging could be evidence of that."

"Possibly," Rosa said. "Or not. It could be just a

strange gift from her lover who is part of a voodoo drug-smuggling ring."

"Or she could've bought it at the flea market in El Pequeño Barrio," Miguel said. "Took a liking to the image with no spiritual reasoning at all."

Rosa shifted in her chair and crossed her legs. "However, her alibi is shaky at best. She says she was with Alex Deleon on the night of Salvador's murder, and I bet you two tickets to see The Platters that he'll say the same thing."

Miguel straightened, his dark eyes sparkling with interest. "The Platters are coming to Santa Bonita? How did I miss that?"

"You've been distracted by your new wife, Detective," Rosa said with a sly grin. "They're playing at the American Legion."

"I really must be living in a love haze." Miguel returned the grin. "Obviously, we have to go."

Rosa cocked her head and said playfully, "Are you asking me out on a date?"

Miguel threw the chalk up in the air and caught it behind his back, "Yes, I am." He pointed it at her.

"Do you also teach biology, Professor el Guapo?" Rosa said dreamily, leaning forward and batting her eyelashes, her elbows on the desk and her fingers interlocked under her chin.

"Stay focused, Mrs. Belmonte, or I'll throw my chalk at you like Miss Lorenzo used to do at me in fourth grade."

"Yes, sir." Rosa pushed a lock of hair out of her eye and sat up straight.

"Miss Lorenzo was my first crush," Miguel added absentmindedly while looking at the blackboard.

"And to think I won your heart without hurling any projectiles at you whatsoever." Rosa sighed, batting her eyelashes again. "I'm sure your hand-writing skills are just as good now as they were then, too," she added, nodding at the board.

"They're actually worse." Miguel stepped around the desk, leaned down, and planted a kiss on Rosa's lips. "I'll take that as a 'yes' for the concert."

"I've already bought tickets."

"Wow. I really have won the lottery with you."

Rosa gently pushed her husband away. "Focus, Detective. Remember? We'll enjoy the concert much more if we solve this case first."

He stroked her chin as he stepped away. "Right. Though, I think I need to keep Sanchez with us in the future. You're far too distracting. I'm tempted to swoop you up and take you home, the heck with my mom." With a breath, he stepped to the board again. "Okay, anything else?"

"If we can find a witness who can positively identify him at the scene of Enrique's murder and then get Allen Fisher to place him at Enrique's house, carrying a gun—that might be enough for a warrant," Rosa said.

"We'd need to canvass the area around the crime scene with a photo," Miguel said. "Maybe someone saw him in the area the day Enrique was killed. If he was arrested before, he has a mugshot somewhere." He looked at his watch. "I contacted Los Angeles precinct when his name came up. Hopefully, we'll get something from them soon."

"Have you searched Simon Rennings' place yet?"

Miguel nodded. "He offered no resistance when I showed up with an officer. We found a Colt .38 among half a dozen other assorted firearms."

"That's interesting," Rosa said. "Had it been fired recently?"

"I have ballistics looking at it. Mr. Rennings swears he hasn't fired it for years. His wife, by the way, corroborates his story of being home shortly after he left the party. Claims he arrived home just after nine. He lives across town."

"Not enough time to shoot Salvador and get home," Rosa observed.

"Nope. If what his wife says is true, he got home

just a few minutes after the fireworks display, which only lasted about three minutes. No way he could have shot Salvador and made it home that fast."

"Off the list for now?" Rosa said.

Miguel marked an *X* beside Rennings' name. "Despite the gun, I think so. I say we concentrate on Alex Deleon and Fabiana Delgado."

"I agree," Rosa said. "Has Dr. Philpott issued a death certificate for Salvador Vasquez yet?"

"No, he hasn't." Miguel let out a frustrated breath. "He has for Enrique, though."

"That's odd."

"No idea what the holdup is. He just says he needs to confirm something, and it'll take another day or so." Miguel took a seat at his desk and removed a sheet of paper from the top drawer. He pushed it toward Rosa.

"The license plate number on the black Ford led us to the name John Smith."

"Fake name, I presume," Rosa said. "Stolen?"

"Not that we know of."

"Alex Deleon must be hiding behind that name."

"Yep, could be one of several aliases."

They turned to the knocking sound on the opened door. An officer stepped in carrying an armful of large leather-bound volumes.

"Sorry to interrupt," he said as he laid them on Miguel's desk. "From LA"

"Thanks, Sam," Miguel said as the officer turned and walked out.

"Okay, here they are." Miguel picked up the first volume in the stack. "Let's get to work."

After leafing through the police records for a couple of hours, they found a picture that matched Rosa's memory of what Alex Deleon looked like, a deep scar on the right cheek confirming it.

Miguel read aloud, "Armondo Bernal alias Raúl Contreras, and I guess now he's Alex Deleon. Arrested in 1950 and served one year for aggravated assault in Los Angeles. Soon after his release, he was arrested again for drug smuggling in Santa Monica. He served four years in California State Penitentiary and was released early last year on probation."

"We need to get Mrs. MacDonald in here, the one who saw Enrique get shot," Rosa said.

"If we get a positive on this picture," Miguel said, "the judge will grant a warrant arrest for the murder of Enrique Vasquez."

*a*lex Deleon sat in the interrogation room, sullenly staring down at the two cloth figurines that lay on the table in front of him. Rosa had positioned herself behind a one-way mirror while Miguel and Detective Sanchez, officially the lead on this case, sat opposite their brooding prisoner. He raised his handcuffed hands to his face—broad and with an expression of contempt and defiance—to brush a long black lock of hair out of his eyes. His snakeskin-cowboy-booted heels bounced on the floor in agitation.

"Nice of you to bring me your little dollies," he said snidely.

"Did you leave these behind in the cars of the Vasquez brothers after you shot them?"

"I never shot anyone, and I've never seen these ugly dolls before in my life. You hombres wouldn't be smoking anything strange, would you?"

"No, but I'll bet *you* would know where we could get some of that stuff," Detective Sanchez said, a dry cigarette hanging from his lips.

Alex Deleon smirked.

"Do you like witchcraft and things of that nature, Mr. Deleon?" Miguel asked. "Maybe know a bruja?"

"You're loco." He lifted his manacled hands in the air and spun his finger while pointing at his temple.

"Las cambiaformas?" Detective Sanchez said.

"Huh?" Alex Deleon looked at Detective Sanchez like he was looking at an alien.

"Ever heard that phrase before?" Detective Sanchez asked.

"Pfft. No."

"I'm going to add it up for you, Mr. Deleon, or Mr. Bernal, or Mr. Contreras or . . . whatever name you're going by right now," Miguel said. "I want to call you *El Pequeño Astuto,* 'the Little Sneaky One,' because of all the drugs you've helped smuggle."

Mr. Deleon glared. "Very funny."

"I like it," Detective Sanchez said, pulling a package of matches from his suit pocket. He lit the cigarette and puffed. "It suits him."

"We know you're involved in the illegal drug trade," Miguel said, "and we know Enrique Vasquez was too. We know you have a history of criminal activity. You've been seen associating with—"

"You got nothing," Alex Deleon interrupted.

Miguel leaned forward on the table. "You should listen closely now, Mr. Deleon. We found your gun, a Colt .38. We are pretty sure it's the same one that killed both Vasquez brothers, and ballistic science will prove it."

Miguel leaned back again, adding casually, "And probably the most damaging of all, Mr. Sneaky, is we have a witness who *saw* you gun down Enrique Vasquez."

His comment was a stretch of the truth, but, of course, Mr. Deleon didn't know that.

Miguel continued. "We have a witness who made a positive identification earlier today from your police mugshot. We also have a witness that saw you on the night of Salvador's murder parked in your car not far from where he was shot, only a few minutes before."

Alex Deleon narrowed his eyes. "The lady in the Plymouth."

Miguel tossed a pen on the table. "We've got you, Mr. Deleon."

"Two murder charges," Detective Sanchez said. His cigarette, now lit, was hanging from his lips. He tugged it out with his thumb and finger and blew smoke in Mr. Deleon's direction. "What do you think the sentence will be for *that*?"

A look of apprehension crossed Alex Deleon's face.

"Here's what I think," Miguel started. "Someone ordered you to kill Enrique for reasons that you would be advised to explain to us since that might buy you some leniency in sentencing. But you followed the wrong car *and* the wrong brother and ended up waiting for him to come out of the party. Now, I don't know how you timed it with the fireworks. Maybe that part was pure coincidence. Anyway, it was dark, and you thought you had the right guy—maybe you didn't even know Enrique had a brother."

Alex Deleon grew extremely agitated—his knees jumped, his head moved side to side, his eyes darted around the room. Rosa guessed he would break soon.

"Then it turns out you hit the wrong man," Miguel said. "After all, they drive the same car and look identical from a distance. Easy mistake to make, but your bosses don't see it that way and get really angry."

"Even though I'm sure they are nice, peace-loving guys," Detective Sanchez added. He tapped ash into a tray, then set his cigarette down, letting a small plume of smoke rise to the ceiling.

"Oh yeah, I bet they are gentle souls who are loyal to their kind," Miguel remarked. "In fact, I bet they have your back right now. They're going to get you the best lawyers. Go the extra mile to save one of their own."

"For sure," Detective Sanchez said, matching Miguel's sarcastic tone. "Those types of guys are like the marines; never leave a man behind."

Like a caged animal, Mr. Deleon's focus darted around the room. He looked at the ceiling then around the room, blinking rapidly and breathing heavily, his olive skin growing redder by the second.

"So, you got a little desperate and shot Enrique in broad daylight," Miguel said. "Like you were Lucky Luciano or something."

"Bugsy Siegel." Detective Sanchez shot Miguel a look. "His guys do stuff like that."

"Wasn't he shot by his girlfriend?" Miguel returned.

"He was. In Las Vegas." Detective Sanchez stared Alex Deleon down. "Girlfriends can be dangerous sometimes."

"Do you have a girlfriend, Mr. Deleon?" Miguel asked.

"She's got nothing to do with this!" Alex Deleon snarled.

Miguel raised his dark eyebrows. "With what?"

There was silence in the room.

Here it comes, Rosa thought, inwardly proud of how Miguel had led the questioning.

Alex Deleon snarled again. "I *didn't* kill the brother!"

"But you did kill Enrique Vasquez," Miguel pressed. "Remember, we've got a witness. Dumb thing to do, in broad daylight like that."

Mr. Deleon's shoulders slumped. His dark eyes flitted back and forth as he made internal calculations. Finally, he said, "I had no choice. They were going to kill me if I didn't." His voice broke as he spoke the damning words.

"You're going to have to eventually give us the names of 'they,' if you want any favors from the prosecution," Miguel said. "But first, tell us why the hit was ordered."

After a long defeated-sounding sigh, Alex Deleon relented. "Enrique wanted to quit the business. It was as simple as that. He announced it two weeks ago. He wanted to find a wife and settle down like his older brother, something stupid like that. Well, you don't just quit this kind of thing. Too many loose ends. He should have known that!

"I didn't even know Salvador was at the party. He's Fabiana's boss, isn't he? What was he even doing there? I was just there to pick up Fabiana." He flashed a weak grin. "Her husband was out of town."

"Mrs. Delgado didn't know you were parked there on the street." Miguel said. "She never mentioned it."

Mr. Deleon shrugged. "I was gonna surprise her."

Miguel took out the picture of Mrs. Delgado's wall hanging.

"Is that from Fabiana's place?" Mr. Deleon asked.

"You've seen it before?" Miguel asked.

"Sure. I was there when Fabiana bought it, down by the marina. It was for sale at a curiosity shop down by the beach. I told her not to waste her money, but she never listens to me."

Miguel gave Alex Deleon a stern look. "Salvador Vasquez was married to my aunt, and I intend to find out who murdered him."

"Hey, I'm sorry for your aunt's loss, amigo, but it wasn't me. I didn't kill anyone that night." Awkwardly, with cuffs rattling, he jabbed a finger at Miguel. "I want a lawyer."

23

The next morning, Rosa drove her Corvette back to El Pequeño Barrio. Mrs. Belmonte wanted to discuss the new wedding plans *again*. Apparently, two bridesmaids weren't enough, and more single girls could qualify. And would she like roses or carnations? Perhaps a bouquet with mixed flowers? And Margarita must be the flower girl, and little Abelardo the ring bearer. What to do about rings? She didn't like it that Rosa and Miguel were wearing them already. What would people think? And then they must discuss food!

Miguel had been correct when he said his mother was loving and kind, but she was also dreadfully exhausting, at least with this blasted wedding!

Rosa pulled onto Camino Coronado, taking deep

breaths to fortify herself, when she saw Consuela Gonzales walking toward a taxi parked in front of her house. Instead of shuffling along like she usually did, Consuela's gait was crisp and purposeful.

Perplexed and curious, Rosa made a quick decision, pulling behind the taxi as it drove away. Mrs. Gonzales had no reason to suspect she was being followed, but Rosa kept a car length back as a precaution. Poor Mrs. Belmonte would have to wait. Hopefully, she wouldn't be too angry at Rosa for missing their date.

Interestingly, the taxi drove straight to the business district—a short five-minute drive—and stopped in front of a real estate office. Rosa parked nearby and watched as Mrs. Gonzales got out of the cab and paid the driver. She walked briskly yet cautiously to the entrance, seemingly, avoiding cracks in the pavement and sidewalk. She held her hand to the side of her face as she moved past the windows before quickly disappearing inside.

Rosa made a quick call to Mrs. Belmonte from the phone booth on the corner, making earnest apologies and promising to come over as soon as she could, before returning to her Corvette to wait on Mrs. Gonzales.

Rosa tapped her fingers on the steering wheel

impatiently. She was about to go inside, pretending to be a potential client, when the taxi returned. The elderly woman must have had the foresight to tell the cabbie to come back in ten minutes. Consuela Gonzales quickly walked out of the office and climbed into the cab, again with her hands shielding her eyes and her gaze downward. The taxi turned around and headed toward the Spanish district.

Should she follow the taxi? Or go inside to see if she could discover what was so important that Mrs. Gonzales had to face all her superstitions to do?

She took a chance and went inside.

After inquiring at the reception desk, Rosa was directed to a middle-aged man in a business suit sitting in a small office that faced the street, a smile on his face. Rosa introduced herself as a concerned friend of Consuela Gonzales, who wanted to apologize for any confusion that might have occurred by her visiting the office.

"I think you've got the wrong Mrs. Gonzales, lady. The Mrs. Gonzales I know is as sharp as a tack!"

"I see," Rosa said. "Clearly, I've underestimated her."

"Oh, yeah," the man said brightly. "She's listing the same house she bought from us last year."

"Is that so," Rosa said, her mind working furiously.

"She's quite a canny lady," the man said with a chuckle. "She negotiated the purchase of the house for a significantly reduced price, made a few improvements to the home, and is now selling it at a tidy profit."

"Where will she live then?" Rosa asked.

"Oh, I'm surprised she didn't tell you. She's moving back to San Felipe as soon as possible. She's hired us to take care of everything, including selling all her furniture and belongings. I think she plans on leaving on the next bus or something." He reached for a card and handed it to Rosa. "Are you in need of a realtor, miss? I'd be happy to help."

"Perhaps in the future," Rosa said. "Thank you."

Rosa walked out of the office feeling bewildered. As she made her way across the street, a thought hit her. She turned around and walked straight to the telephone booth on the corner, dug out her notes, and flipped through the pages until she found what she was looking for.

"Hello, Master Sergeant Cummings, this is Rosa Reed. I came out to your shooting range yesterday."

"Oh, good! I was hoping you would call. Have you given some thought to getting a membership?

We would love to have a woman with your shooting skills here. I'm sure it would attract other women over time."

"Perhaps, but I'm actually calling about something else. You mentioned an 'older gal' who came out occasionally."

"Oh yes, a sweet little old lady. She's a pretty good shot for someone of her advanced age. She takes a taxi out here about once a week and stays for an hour. Doesn't say much, but she sure shoots up a storm. I'd hate to have her angry with me."

"Do you mind giving me her name?"

"Why? She didn't shoot anyone, did she?" The man chuckled heartily. "Hang on; I forget her last name. The Spanish ones are hard for me to remember. I'll have to look it up. I know her first name is Camilla or . . ."

"Consuela?" Rosa said. "Consuela Gonzales?"

"Bingo. That's it."

Rosa thanked him, hung up, and hurriedly dialed the number of the Santa Bonita Police Department. Thirty seconds later, she was racing to her car.

24

Twenty minutes later, Rosa sat in her car in front of Consuela Gonzales' house. She was just six doors down and around the corner from the home of Maria Belmonte and right next to the lot that was the scene of the murder of Salvador Vasquez. She had made one stop on the way from the real estate office, finding what she was looking for at a nearby general store.

While Rosa waited for Miguel, she drove slowly down the back alley where she had taken photographs the morning after the murder, calculating the time it would have taken to walk the distance from Mrs. Belmonte's backyard to the empty lot.

Miguel arrived in an unmarked police car and

stepped out, carrying a small briefcase. He stared quizzically at Rosa as she approached. "Are you sure about this?" he said.

Rosa stared straight ahead. "I think so. But we'll find out easily enough if I'm wrong."

"We'll either need a confession or to find the weapon to make an arrest. I couldn't get a warrant on such short notice." Miguel exhaled. "We don't even have a motive."

"She could be gone by the time you get a warrant," Rosa said. "She's making plans to leave soon. I don't know what the motive is, but I intend to find out."

They knocked on the front door and waited. After a few moments, the door cracked open slowly, allowing only a few inches for them to see the diminutive form of Consuela Gonzales peering suspiciously at them with her shining, small eyes.

"Hello, Mrs. Gonzales," Miguel said. "I'm Maria Belmonte's son. Do you remember me?"

"No," she answered in a fragile voice.

Rosa remembered their short conversation at the party. "Mrs. Gonzales, I'm Rosa Reed. We met at the fiesta, little Margarita's birthday party."

Mrs. Gonzales stared blankly, and Rosa admired the woman's acting skills. After another long moment, she wordlessly opened the door far enough for them to come in.

The house was neatly organized and smelled like Pine-Sol. Someone had been cleaning up.

Looking for any wall hangings or strange-looking paintings like had been found in Fabiana Delgado's place, Rosa glanced around the room. She saw nothing out of the ordinary. It was just a typical house with clean, relatively modern furniture, suggesting it had been bought new just a few years earlier. The only suspicious thing about it was that it was not what one would have expected when visiting the house of an old lady suffering from a dementia illness.

Consuela Gonzales shuffled unsteadily over to the living room couch and slowly lowered herself onto one of the upholstered chairs. Gone was her quick and purposeful gait.

Rosa and Miguel sat together on the couch. Across from them, Consuela Gonzales stared back with a confused look while saying nothing.

"*Lo siento,*" Miguel started as he put his briefcase on the coffee table. "We hate to bother you."

"I have chocolates!" Her voice suddenly brightened as her eyes snapped open. "You always loved chocolates!" She struggled to rise from her seat.

"No, no, that's okay," Miguel said, motioning for her to stay seated. He patted his stomach and smiled. "I'm trying not to get fat like my brother."

"I don't have those little macadamia pieces you always ate when you were small," Mrs. Gonzales said. Her wrinkled face showed sudden disappointment as she settled back into her chair.

Losing patience with the charade, Rosa reached into her bag. "You look very nice today, Mrs. Gonzales," she said.

"Gracias," the old lady said, her eyes narrowing with suspicion.

"Especially your hair," Rosa said. "You must have taken a lot of time with it today."

Mrs. Gonzales idly put her hand up to her graying hair. "Oh, *no lo sé . . .*"

"Here, have a look." Rosa pulled out a six-inch by eight-inch vanity mirror she had found at the store and turned it toward the elderly woman.

"Put that away!" Mrs. Gonzales shrieked, shielding her face with her hand.

"What's the matter?" Rosa asked calmly. "It's just a harmless mirror." She held it closer to Mrs. Gonzales, taking no pleasure in seeing the old lady's panic, but it had to be done.

"Get out!" Mrs. Gonzales yelled as she quickly

stood up, still covering her face. "Get out before you regret it!" Her voice was powerful, and she emanated anger and fierceness. All signs of frailty were gone, and the transformation was unsettling.

"It's all right," Rosa said as she turned the mirror to face toward herself and held it close to her chest. Miguel stood and blocked the way out of the living room.

"I hear you're leaving us soon," Rosa said calmly. "Going back to San Felipe?"

"How did you know that?" Mrs. Gonzales said, crumpling into herself again as she plopped onto the couch.

"I don't have any special powers like una cambi-aformas, but I *am* a detective, Mrs. Gonzales."

The old woman slowly turned herself toward Rosa, her gaze as cold as death. Miguel opened the briefcase and pulled out one of the strange figurines they had found at both murder scenes.

Mrs. Gonzales blanched.

"Quite skilfully made," Rosa said. "I'm not sure how you got this into Enrique Vasquez's car, but we'll find out. I'm just wondering . . . if we searched your house right now, would we find some of these colorful rags? Or perhaps a spool of black thread? How about artwork depicting a creature who is half woman and half moth?"

The old woman scowled, the many lines in her forehead deepening. "That would prove nothing!"

"How about a gun?" Miguel said. "Or maybe you tossed it already. I think we have enough to—"

"You have *nothing*," Mrs. Gonzales spat.

"I have this nice mirror," Rosa said as she turned it once again toward Mrs. Gonzales.

"Ahhh, put it away! Put it awaaaay."

"Why?" Rosa asked. "Did you command a spirit to do something for you? I think it would like to make your acquaintance."

"All right, all right!" Mrs. Gonzales' brown eyes flashed with fear.

Rosa quickly turned the mirror back around the other way. This was the strangest method of getting a confession she'd ever used.

"I can escape any prison anyway." Mrs. Gonzales patted her hair as she calmed herself, reassured when Rosa put the mirror back in her purse.

"Of course you can," Miguel said. "So why not tell us everything?"

"It was their time, the Vasquez men," Mrs. Gonzales said, straightening herself on the chair. "It was prophesied by the reading of the moon cycles long ago in San Felipe. This month, this week. It had to be done."

"Why?" Rosa asked.

"When I was a young woman in San Felipe, still new to the ways of la bruja, I fell in love with a young businessman named Carlos Vasquez. He promised to marry me. We would have been happy, but then he broke his promise and fled the country with another woman." Her black eyes flashed. Two days later, my brother Juan, his wife, and two kids died in a terrible house fire. It was a sign. Fire has symbolic meaning for someone who is un cambiaformas. When someone close to you dies in a fire, it means that the spirits have come into your household through a spiritual breach. This breach is caused when someone betrays you. It was clear to me that the fire happened because of Carlos's betrayal of me."

Mrs. Gonzales' wrinkled face pursed like a dried-up apple. "On that day, I put a curse on all the future sons of Carlos Vasquez. I learned the ways of la cambiaformas and became a fully fledged bruja to fulfill the curse." Her eyes glittered with hate. "When I learned the sons had moved to America, I followed them and waited until the prophesied time came."

"Posing as a woman with dementia," Rosa said.

"I am una cambiaformas."

"You lied to my mother about your health," Miguel said. "She cared for you."

Consuela Gonzales scowled at him. "Your mother doesn't know how to be suspicious. She thinks kindness is a strength. She thinks only with her heart. Bah, she was easy to fool. I bought this house when I learned that a Vasquez had married into the family down the street. Soliciting sympathy was a ruse to get invited over to family gatherings."

"How did you time it so well with the fireworks?" Miguel asked.

"When you are on a sacred mission and the time is right, the *figurilla,* along with the dark spirit in the mirror, will help you. When I saw Salvador leaving, just as the fireworks were about to start, I knew it was time. I flew like a moth to where I saw he had parked his car. My kitchen window overlooks the lot, you see." She pointed toward the north end of the house. "I had my gun with me, of course, ready at all times. It didn't take me long to get to the vacant lot."

Rosa caught Miguel's look. That was the confession they needed, with both Miguel and herself as witnesses.

"What is your connection with Enrique?" Rosa asked. "We know you didn't kill him."

"No, I didn't," Mrs. Gonzales laughed. Not a cackle as one would expect from a witch, but more like an old rusty gate swinging on its hinges.

It sent a shiver down Rosa's spine.

Mrs. Gonzales continued. "When you are on a sacred quest, and the time has been so long in coming, sometimes the spirit in the mirror will come to your aid in a way that is not even imagined." She glanced furtively down at Rosa's purse, her mouth twitching. "In the night, I put the figurine in Enrique's car while it was parked in front of his house. It is an easy thing to do for una cambiaformas. When I heard that he had been killed the next day, I offered many prayers of thanks to the spirit in the mirror."

"We'll see how your shape-shifting powers work in jail," Miguel said as he got to his feet. "I'm placing you under arrest for the murder of Salvador Vasquez."

25

The Santa Bonita Veterans' Theater wasn't as packed as when Elvis Presley had been there, but there was still a large crowd, though not so young or boisterous. The Platters had had several hits on the radio, and Rosa found their music comfortable and melodic to listen to.

The wood floor of the auditorium was flat and could be used as a dance floor, but tonight it was filled with rolling risers filled with collapsible, vinyl-covered chairs. Rosa and Miguel took their reserved seats at the end of a row near the front of one of the sloped seating sections.

"The show starts in fifteen minutes." Miguel glanced at his watch. "I hope Carlotta and Sanchez aren't going to miss the beginning."

There were two reserved chairs right beside Rosa. It was the first time the two couples had "double-dated," and Rosa looked forward to it. Perhaps Miguel had finally warmed up to his burly partner dating his sister.

"I told ya we'd make it in time, Carlotta," Detective Sanchez said as he and Carlotta appeared, looking for their seats.

Detective Sanchez pointed to Rosa and Miguel with the program brochure in one hand and ticket stubs in the other. He wore a crisply ironed, blue-collared shirt, beige pleated trousers held up with black suspenders, and black-and-white wingtip oxford shoes. His black, wiry hair was nicely combed and slicked back perfectly.

Rosa had never seen him dressed so snappily. She had to admit, he looked rather handsome. She noted that he still sported his trademark cigarette stub hanging from the corner of his mouth, though.

Some things took more time.

As usual, Carlotta was dressed in bold colors. A purple crinoline peeked out from her full skirt.

"You didn't get the news?" Detective Sanchez said to Miguel as the couple settled into their seats, Carlotta's shoulder next to Rosa's.

"What news?" Miguel asked.

"You left the office just before Dr. Philpott called. Are you ready for this? Consuela Gonzales did *not* murder Salvador Vasquez."

"What? Of course she did," Miguel said. "We have a full confession!"

"Nope. Philpott apologized that it took so long to confirm it, but it wasn't a bullet that killed Salvador Vasquez. He suffered a massive heart attack. Philpott says it happened probably just moments before he was shot."

Another strange twist in this rather bizarre case.

"I can't wait to see how the District Attorney handles this one!" Detective Sanchez said with a hoot. "The old lady will no doubt see the inside of a jail cell, but they're going to have to get creative for the charges. Casting an evil spell without a license? Smuggling illegal hoochie koochie over the border?" He chuckled. "Or wait, I know: conspiracy to ruin a kid's birthday party. *That* oughta get her at least five to ten years, depending on the judge."

"I see you've really given this a lot of thought," Miguel said.

Detective Sanchez grinned, catching the cigarette stub as it fell from his lips. "There ain't no stopping a creative mind like mine, amigo."

"She could be charged for desecrating a corpse,"

Rosa said. "Or perhaps they can try attempted murder."

Not for the first time since the arrest of Consuela Gonzales had Rosa wondered about what kind of person it would take to cast a curse on someone and then have the twisted determination to see it through many decades—when the "prophecy" was to be fulfilled.

Rosa had been in the interrogation room when Consuela Gonzales had fully confessed to the police late the previous night. By Consuela's own admission, she had never married and had used the term "Mrs." as part of her lifelong disguise. She was so set on her hateful quest, she moved to America, even though she could have lived a comfortable life in Mexico due to shrewd real estate ventures that had earned her a small fortune.

A wasted, brilliant mind.

Instead, her strange, lifelong agenda had caused her to do unthinkable things. To sit at a child's birthday party, eagerly waiting for the right moment to sneak through an unwatched gate and shoot someone through the head, all done while children laughed and celebrated just a few hundred feet away —these were not the actions of a sound mind.

Consuela Gonzales had been so driven by

vengeance, she fabricated a fake life, a ruse she had maintained to the utmost degree, even going so far as to feign a dementia illness that fooled everyone. But perhaps a sort of mental illness had already begun a long time ago.

Rosa glanced at Carlotta and took a double-take. Were those tears in her friend's eyes? She leaned in to whisper, "Is everything all right? You seem down."

Carlotta tried to smile, but it seemed to make her eyes leak more. The house lights had dimmed by that point, and neither Miguel nor Detective Sanchez had noticed the tears streaming down her cheeks.

Rosa handed Carlotta a fresh tissue.

Carlotta answered, "I'm in a bit of trouble, Rosa."

When a girl used the word "trouble," it usually meant one thing. Rosa squeezed Carlotta's hand. "Bill loves you. It's going to be all right."

"I know, but we need to get married soon, and well, you and Miguel are ahead of us in line. And I can't tell Mamá; I just can't." She sighed. "I don't know how we'll avoid a scandal."

Even a voluptuous woman like Carlotta couldn't hide a pregnancy for long, and then there was the timing of a child's birth after the wedding that would be up for speculation. Drat. If Mrs.

Belmonte wasn't insisting Rosa herself and Miguel have a second ceremony, Carlotta and Detective Sanchez could be the ones getting married the next month.

Perhaps they still could.

"Carlotta," Rosa began. "I have an idea. How would you like to have a double wedding?"

Carlotta's brown eyes formed huge circles. "You'd do that?"

"I would." In fact, Rosa would prefer it. A double wedding would mean she wouldn't be the whole focus, and if the bishop failed them, the ceremony wouldn't be a complete sham. The priest would bless at least one couple. "Please say you'll do it."

"Oh, Rosa!" Carlotta threw her arms around Rosa, surrounding her in a pleasant jasmine fragrance.

"What's goin' on with you two?" Detective Sanchez asked.

"Oh, honey, I have a big surprise for you," Carlotta said.

But before she could get into it, the emcee entered the stage to appreciative applause.

Miguel caught Rosa's eyes, and she mouthed, "I'll tell you later."

The lights over the audience went dark, and the

emcee shouted, "Ladies and gentlemen, I present The Platters!"

Four tuxedo-clad and handsome black men, along with an attractive black woman wearing a white evening gown, stepped into the spotlight. They quickly gathered around a single microphone and smiled broadly as the band played a musical introduction recognized by millions of radio listeners across America.

With a warm, delightful croon, the male lead singer began, "Oh-oh yes, I'm the great pretender."

If you enjoyed reading *Murder at the Fiesta* please help others enjoy it too.

Recommend it: Help others find the book by recommending it to friends, readers' groups, discussion boards.

Suggest it: to your local library.

Review it: Please tell other readers why you liked this book by reviewing it on Amazon or Goodreads.

** Please don't add spoilers to your review. **

WHAT'S NEXT?

MURDER AT THE WEDDINGS
A Rosa Reed Mystery #10

Seeing double is murder!

If one wedding is good, a double wedding is better! Rosa and Miguel agree that walking down the aisle with Bill and Carlotta solves a lot of social and familial problems, but the drama is notched up when a dead body arrives with dessert!

Don't miss this final installment of a Rosa Reed Mystery series where Rosa finally gets her happily ever after.

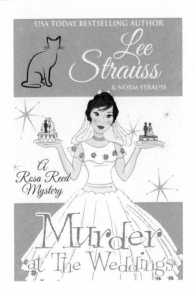

Buy on AMAZON or read for free with Kindle
Unlimited!

*Rosa & Miguel's Wartime Romance is a BONUS short
story* exclusively for Lee's newsletter subscribers.

Subscribe Now!

Read on for excerpt.

Don't miss the next Ginger Gold Mystery!

MURDER AT THE SAVOY

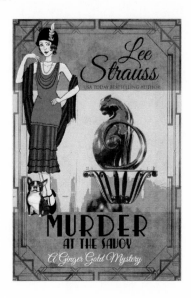

Murder's frightfully unlucky!

Mrs. Ginger Reed, known also as Lady Gold, settles into home life with her husband Chief Inspector Basil Reed, son Scout and newborn daughter Rosa, but when an opportunity to join a dinner party at the renowned Savoy Hotel if offered, she's eager to engage in a carefree night with friends. Some of the guests are troubled when their party's number lands at unlucky thirteen, as death is sure to come to the first person who leaves the table.

Thankfully, the Savoy has an answer to this superstitious dilemma. A small statue of a black cat fondly known as Kaspar is given the empty seat, rounding the number to fourteen.

Unfortunately, in this instance Kaspar didn't fulfill his duties and a murder is committed. The case is tricky and complicated by a recent escape of a prisoner who has a bone to pick with Basil. Are the two seemingly unrelated incidents connected?

Ginger and Basil work together to solve one while avoiding the other, and what can they do about the black cat who crossed their path?

Buy on AMAZON or read for free with Kindle Unlimited!

ROSA & MIGUEL'S WARTIME ROMANCE

PREQUEL - EXCERPT

Rosa Reed first laid eyes on Miguel Belmonte on the fourteenth day of February in 1945. She was a senior attending a high school dance, and he a soldier who played in the band.

She'd been dancing with her date, Tom Hawkins, a short, stalky boy with pink skin and an outbreak of acne, but her gaze continued to latch onto the bronze-skinned singer, with dark crew-cut hair, looking very dapper in a black suit.

In a life-changing moment, their eyes locked. Despite the fact that she stared at the singer over the shoulder of her date, she couldn't help the bolt of electricity that shot through her, and when the singer smiled—and those dimples appeared—heavens, her knees almost gave out!

"Rosa?"

Tom's worried voice brought her back to reality. "Are you okay? You went a little limp there. Do you feel faint? It is mighty hot in here." Tom released Rosa's hand to tug at his tie. "Do you want to get some air?"

Rosa felt a surge of alarm. Invitations to step outside the gymnasium were often euphemisms to get fresh.

In desperation she searched for her best friend Nancy Davidson—her best *American* friend, that was. Vivien Eveleigh claimed the position of *best* friend back in London, and Rosa missed her. Nancy made for a sufficient substitute. A pretty girl with honey-blond hair, Nancy, fortunately, was no longer dancing, and was sitting alone.

"I think I'll visit the ladies, Tom, if you don't mind."

He looked momentarily put out, then shrugged. "Suit yourself." He joined a group of lads—boys—at the punch table, and joined in with their raucous laughter. Rosa didn't want to know what they were joking about, or at whose expense.

Nancy understood Rosa's plight as she wasn't entirely pleased with her fellow either. "If only you and I could dance with each other."

"One can't very well go to a dance without a date, though," Rosa said.

Nancy laughed. "*One* can't."

Rosa rolled her eyes. Even after four years of living in America, her Englishness still manifested when she was distracted.

And tonight's distraction was the attractive lead singer in the band, and shockingly, he seemed to have sought her face out too.

Nancy had seen the exchange and gave Rosa a firm nudge. "No way, José. I know he's cute, but he's from the wrong side of the tracks. Your aunt would have a conniption."

Nancy wasn't wrong about that. Aunt Louisa had very high standards, as one who was lady of Forrester mansion, might.

"I'm only looking!"

Nancy harrumphed. "As long as it stays that way."

Continue reading >>>

Subscribe Now!

MORE FROM LEE STRAUSS

On AMAZON

THE ROSA REED MYSTERIES

(1950s cozy historical)

Murder at High Tide

Murder on the Boardwalk

Murder at the Bomb Shelter

Murder on Location

Murder and Rock 'n Roll

Murder at the Races

Murder at the Dude Ranch

Murder in London

Murder at the Fiesta

Murder at the Weddings

GINGER GOLD MYSTERY SERIES (cozy 1920s historical)

Cozy. Charming. Filled with Bright Young Things. This Jazz Age murder mystery will entertain and delight you with its 1920s flair and pizzazz!

LADY GOLD INVESTIGATES (Ginger Gold companion short stories)

Volume 1

Volume 2

Volume 3

Volume 4

HIGGINS & HAWKE MYSTERY SERIES (cozy 1930s historical)

The 1930s meets Rizzoli & Isles in this friendship depression era cozy mystery series.

Death at the Tavern

Death on the Tower

Death on Hanover

Death by Dancing

A NURSERY RHYME MYSTERY SERIES(mystery/sci fi)

Marlow finds himself teamed up with intelligent and savvy Sage Farrell, a girl so far out of his league he feels blinded in her presence - literally - damned glasses! Together they work to find the identity of @gingerbreadman. Can they stop the killer before he strikes again?

Gingerbread Man

Life Is but a Dream

Hickory Dickory Dock

Twinkle Little Star

LIGHT & LOVE (sweet romance)

Set in the dazzling charm of Europe, follow Katja, Gabriella, Eva, Anna and Belle as they find strength, hope and love.

Love Song

Your Love is Sweet

In Light of Us

Lying in Starlight

PLAYING WITH MATCHES (WW2 history/romance)

A sobering but hopeful journey about how one young German boy copes with the war and propaganda. Based on true events.

A Piece of Blue String (companion short story)

THE CLOCKWISE COLLECTION (YA time travel romance)

Casey Donovan has issues: hair, height and uncontrollable trips to the 19th century! And now this ~ she's accidentally taken

Nate Mackenzie, the cutest boy in the school, back in time.
Awkward.

Clockwise

Clockwiser

Like Clockwork

Counter Clockwise

Clockwork Crazy

Clocked (companion novella)

Standalones

Seaweed

Love, Tink

ABOUT THE AUTHORS

Lee Strauss is a USA TODAY bestselling author of The Ginger Gold Mysteries series, The Higgins & Hawke Mystery series, The Rosa Reed Mystery series (cozy historical mysteries), A Nursery Rhyme Mystery series (mystery suspense), The Light & Love series (sweet romance), The Clockwise Collection (YA time travel romance), and young adult historical fiction with over a million books read. She has titles published in German, Spanish and French, and a growing audio library.

When Lee's not writing or reading she likes to cycle, hike, and watch the ocean. She loves to drink caffè lattes and red wines in exotic places, and eat dark chocolate anywhere.

Norm Strauss is a singer-songwriter and performing artist who's seen the stage of The Voice of Germany. Cozy mystery writing is a new passion he shares with his wife Lee Strauss. Check out Norm's music page www.normstrauss.com

For more info on books by Lee Strauss and her social media links, visit leestraussbooks.com. To make sure you don't miss the next new release, be sure to sign up for her readers' list!

Did you know you can follow your favorite authors on Bookbub? If you subscribe to Bookbub — (and if you don't, why don't you? - They'll send you daily emails alerting you to sales and new releases on just the kind of books you like to read!) — follow me to make sure you don't miss the next Ginger Gold Mystery!

www.leestraussbooks.com
leestraussbooks@gmail.com